# Hope

### Hive Honey Quest, Volume 1

Amarah Parks

Published by Amarah Parks LLC, 2024.

HOPE

**First edition. May 6, 2024.**

Copyright © 2024 Amarah Parks.

ISBN: 979-8223886181

Written by Amarah Parks.

# Table of Contents


Chapter 1: A Doomed Queen ........................................................1

Chapter 2: Special Delivery ......................................................5

Chapter 3: Nearly Death .........................................................12

Chapter 4: The Prophecy and the Egg .............................................17

Chapter 5: Hope is Born .........................................................23

Chapter 6: The Daydream .........................................................27

Chapter 7: The Daughters Return .................................................32

Chapter 8: First Progresses in Secrecy ..........................................38

Chapter 9: The Wild Hive ........................................................45

Chapter 10: The Honeycrystal ....................................................53

Chapter 11: Hope is Found .......................................................58

Chapter 12: Unfolding ...........................................................64

Chapter 13: Soldiers ............................................................70

Chapter 14: Warplan .............................................................75

Chapter 15: Where is Royal? .....................................................81

Chapter 16: Devastated ..........................................................84

Chapter 17: Sideways ............................................................86

Chapter 18: Theo's Rebellion ....................................................90

Chapter 19: Buzzz Must Leave ....................................................95

Chapter 20: And There Was Peace .................................................99

I dedicate this book to my parents who decided to try out homeschooling and unit studies. Thanks to their decision, I had more time and energy to pour into my passion projects. I also dedicate it to 12 year olds around the world who, like my 12 year old self did when writing the original copy of this book, dream of one day becoming published writers.

# HOPE By: Amarah Parks

# Chapter 1: A Doomed Queen

"Wake up Madam, you've laid an egg!"

A tired queen bee shifted out of a deep sleep, blinking in confusion. It was just another day in the hive, and she wasn't used to being alerted after laying an egg. She laid eggs all the time, and usually they were swiftly packed away into a nursery comb to safely develop. *Perhaps something is wrong?* As her eyesight cleared, she realized the small, confined space she was in. *Wait, where am I?* Tiny strands of light riddled her face through a strange wire mesh which wrapped around a thin, wooden frame. She peered toward the rays, aware that she was definitely not in her hive anymore. Her body stiffened. "What's wrong... where are we?"

"Um... I believe we are... well..."

"Well tell me, before our honey goes bad!" Royal forced a lighthearted joke, trying to keep her demeanor level despite her alarm. After all, she knew it was her duty as a queen to remain calm and collected. "Tell me what you know."

"Your Highness, I seem to remember some odd events. It all happened so fast... The Honeybandits were after you, and we tried our best to stay near. Then, smoke started to billow, and I don't remember much after that. Before we knew it, we were coming to awareness, trapped in this wooden box!" The tiny bee who had been speaking shuddered in distress. "Everything outside here smells foreign. I think we've been plucked from our hive."

Royal's heart sank. She closed her eyes and took a deep breath. Opening them, she scanned the group of bees in the box with her. *Love, Trust, Peace, Faith, and Nectar, my little nurse bee.* These were just a few of her cherished daughters. A pang of sadness pierced Royal as the reality set in. So many of her beloved offspring remained back home, and she would probably never see them again. She knew what was happening. She and her friends were being transported, likely to a new hive who needed a seasoned queen.

"Your Majesty," Peace interrupted her thoughts with a feeble voice, "Based on the direction we've been going, I believe we may be taking your mother's place in... Hive Honey Quest."

A chilling silence filled the space. Royal held back a gasp. *Hive Honey Quest...* Hive Honey Quest was known for its high levels of honey production, and its large, resilient bees. However, having been born there, Royal knew of its terrors. She had warned her offspring of their twisted ways... things that defied nature and normalcy. There, drones had unnaturally long lives. They were dangerous, believing themselves superior, and sought power with an unmatched hunger. Royal kept her fear mostly concealed, but she was terrified for herself, her workers, and her new egg. *If that is truly our destination, will we even survive there?*

Hive Honey Quest was far from home, but not too far for a Honeybandit's machine to cover in a few hours. Royal edged her way to the wall, peering through the mesh, to try to identify landmarks nearby. Before her was a memorable scene that confirmed her fears. The treeline, the fields, the species of flowers, and the smell of the air - It was all so familiar. *Well, this is definitely the place.* A chill traveled down her spine as she turned to the girls, downcast. They looked at her with urgent expressions. Taking a breath to compose herself, she glanced around the box that carried them. "What is the situation when it comes to this box?"

"There is a candy-coated entrance, but we can't quite access it. I don't know what to do!" Nectar paused gravely. She and the other workers huddled together for a sense of safety. After several quiet moments, she proceeded with caution. "Is everything you've said about Hive Honey Quest true? I don't know how we could bear to live there..." her voice trailed off.

Royal nodded slowly, her face reflecting her troubled thoughts. It seemed undeniable that Hive Honey Quest was their intended destination, and she knew that boxes like this could not be escaped quickly from the inside. "Girls, I believe we are on our way to Hive Honey Quest, and you must be reminded of the dangers we may face." She looked at each of her friends solemnly. "You know how things work at home - drones live to be fathers, but rarely meet their offspring. They live short and purposeful lives. They do not carry high rank, and have no other interest but to serve the hive. But where we are headed, it's different." She paused. "Drones there are able to live much longer, and are of great size and strength. Because of this, they hold much more power. You should be careful to not be alone with one, as he will easily crush you if he so wishes. With such long lives and few quests, these drones are particularly power hungry, and seem to breed conflict and deception. While there is an illusion of the usual Queen rule, do not be fooled. The drones have the final say."

"Who knows how they treat their queen!" Love blurted out, holding back tears. "How will we know that you are safe?" Every worker bee's greatest task was to protect their queen, and Love was no exception.

"I don't know if things are different than before, but we *should* be capable of staying in contact no matter what happens," Royal nodded reassuringly.

"What else do we need to know?" Faith was trying to be composed, but was clearly shaken.

Royal sighed. "Girls, Hive Honey Quest does not honor Lighthive. We may be unable to speak of our faith there if we want to live harmoniously. Do not forsake your hearts, but for a time, it would be wise to be cautious. You shouldn't speak of it openly. As for the drones, they aren't hard to spot, even from afar. They are usually adorned with honey crystals, pollen, or beeswax as ornaments of vanity. Despite their flashy garb, you must know that they are also masterfully sneaky. You should expect that one may be beevesdropping on you at any given moment."

Nectar's face was twisted in concern. "Are you certain there is no escape from this fate? I can check again..."

"Unfortunately, we have no choice. I have been in a box like this before. It isn't made to be broken through quickly. We can't be far from Hive Honey Quest now. When we arrive, we will be placed directly into the hive, and the workers there will free us from the outside. I'm not sure what kind of welcome we will have, but we can only pray for favor." Royal smiled weakly, gathering her daughters into a warm huddle.

The company fell into a solemn vigil. In one day, their entire existence had changed. This displacement would bring a peril they had hoped to never experience, but there was no running from it. Royal was mournful as she prepared herself for this hardship. Fear pierced her like a twig. She looked down at the brand new egg she cradled in her arms. *To start a fresh new life in a place like that... It isn't right.* Royal decided that this egg would not leave her side until it hatched. She closed her eyes and let out a long breath. Visions of the life they'd been ripped from filled her mind, and her face became hot with tears. *Oh, I wish we were home!*

# Chapter 2: Special Delivery

Hive Honey Quest was grand indeed. It was surrounded by the trees of a coniferous forest at the edge of a meadow. The domestic hive was housed in a few large, white crates fashioned out of wood. They were stacked at least three crates high, and each one held several frames for bees to store honey and brood. There were also many bee-cells to reside in, a lavish but cozy throne room for the queen, and a spacious area near the hive entrance called the landing grounds. Everything was organized, uniform, and purposeful. The hive was always buzzing with activity, and everybee worked very hard to accomplish whatever was needed.

Lilac was the current Queen of the hive. She and her mate were together in her throne room, which was softly lit and filled with luxury items. "I want to speak to my daughter immediately, so I can share a few tidbits about our lovely hive," Lilac buzzed, shifting excitedly in her cushioned chair. She was an old queen with graying fur, but still looked large and strong. No matter her strength, she seemed to refuse to stand or walk. Instead, she expected to be carried. Her expression was full of pride and privilege. Her messenger bee - called Bebee - had sighted the Honeybandits as they transported the box toward the hive on foot. This meant that the young queen would arrive any minute. She kept shifting in her chair with dramatic impatience.

"Of course, my dear," a terrible drone answered, his deep voice laced with subtle mockery. This particular drone was adorned with beeswax ornaments, and had carefully placed pollen clumps on his furry coat. The yellow beads cascaded in a diagonal pattern and proudly extended down his entire thorax. He stood tall and strong, larger than any other drone in the hive, and his presence was truly unsettling.

"I will miss you, my friend, my king, when I am to pass..." Lilac stammered in a sweet tone, then added, "Who have you selected as prince? Who will reign the hive with you, and be Royal's mate, my dearest Buzzz? He should be strong and resilient of course."

"I think Sting will do the best to honor your daughter, and be her mate," Buzzz answered, sure of his choice. He gently shook his furry coat, and it shimmered as it reflected the light from golden lamps. "He will make an excellent deputy. I've put special time into training him for such a position."

"That seems about right," the queen nodded in approval. Sighing, she scanned the doorway with growing frustration. "Now where is everyone? I must be first to speak to the arrivals! Honey?" She panted emphatically as she recovered from the mild strain of raising her voice.

Just in time, Honey and six other workers filed into the room. Honey was Lilac's nurse bee, and was never far away as Lilac's days were coming to an end. The workers surrounded her quickly, preparing to lift.

"Are you feeling okay?" Honey eyed her queen, genuinely concerned. Her high-pitched voice was polite, but grating.

"Honestly? I'm feeling *dead*, you deerfly!" Lilac snapped, glaring at the nurse bee irritably for a few moments. "All I need you to do right now is to carry me." She sighed, then muttered, "Just get me to the landing grounds on time." She resumed her queenly poise as she waited.

"Your Majesty." Honey dipped her head and got straight to work. It was commonplace for Lilac to address her workers differently than the drones. She usually only spoke with true respect toward her King, Buzzz. It seemed that she either disliked or hated everyone else. All seven bees placed their hands under the large queen to hoist her. At the count of three, they lifted with some difficulty at first, but then gained their balance. For the next few minutes they precariously began their trek weaving through hallways and rooms to get to the front of the hive.

The landing grounds were wide open, allowing for a great crowd of bees to convene, and it was usually abuzz with activity. Today was no exception. The room was all hustle and bustle, with no sense of today being different than any other day. The workers set their queen down at the edge of the crowd, panting.

It wasn't long before the passersby recognized that their queen was nearby. A few doctor bees rushed to Lilac's side. One spoke, "Your Highness, we have begun treating a few select eggs so that they may compete for leadership of the hive. Only a few more days on the royal jelly, and..." She was cut off abruptly with a hiss.

"Absolutely not! No more royal jelly." Lilac scowled harshly at the crew. The room began to fall silent as the queen spoke. "We have a new queen coming who is ready at once to start the task!" Shock fell onto the doctor bee's faces, followed by grief. All of the eggs they had been treating would now need to be discarded entirely.

The doctor bees' concerns were quickly dismissed as the crowd began to process this news. They buzzed quietly amongst themselves. Some seemed disappointed that there would be no queen games, which were certainly great fun. Others seemed intrigued and excited about the mysterious newcomer.

"Who is it?" A drone cried.

"How do you know?" Another called.

Letting out a sigh, Lilac composed herself as the crowd waited in anticipation. She projected, "My messenger, Bebee, sent information that my young daughter, Royal, is arriving at this very moment. She will inherit the crown in Hive Honey Quest when I pass. She will be your Queen!"

Cheers of approval and fascination arose from the crowd, as bees shook their wings and abdomens. A few of the older workers and drones had known Royal before she was shipped off, while briefly. Lilac relaxed, satisfied, as the hive communicated the news with each other.

A group of drones nearby whooped in excitement. Lilac turned their way with a mischievous smile. "They think they'll have a shot at seducing the new queen." She laughed. Then, amongst the drones at the edge of the crowd, she spotted the modestly adorned drone named Thistle. He was standing guard next to his burly brother Theo at the hive's entrance. Her eyes hardened with disgust. Thistle wasn't as large as most of the drones in the hive, nor was he as resilient.

The old queen scoffed, leaning over to quietly murmur to her king, "Thistle doesn't deserve to dwell in this hive, much less guard it. He is one of the weakest drones we have, and is showing ghastly signs of age. It's simply unacceptable. He should be promptly stripped of his title." Buzzz nodded, glancing sourly at the drone. Thistle had many traits similar to drones of other "weak" hives, and the two believed he carried undesirable and unworthy genetics. "How do Thistle and Theo share the same bloodline? Anyway, remind me to deal with him as soon as the new arrivals have settled in."

"We ought to send Thistle off in exile. It would be best to ensure the strength of the hive for generations to come." Buzzz nodded toward the unsuspecting drone hopefully.

"Yes, yes. But first, I want everyone ready to welcome my daughter." Lilac then added, "I must make sure she is ready to do an excellent job here. She may need a lot of guidance..." The old queen paused to catch her breath after all of the discourse.

Buzzz hesitated, about to push the issue. Instead, he added, "Theo, on the other hand, has truly impressed me. He is shaping up to be a fine drone, strong and focused." The two looked at Theo, acknowledging his stature and expression.

"You're right. At least something of value came from my tireless egg-laying." Lilac sighed dramatically, bored of the subject. As if on cue, Bebee burst into the hive once again and the buzz of activity in the clearing paused to listen intently.

"Special delivery! Make room!"

A blinding light flashed as the hive was opened with a rumble, and a strange wooden box was lowered perfectly into the center of the landing grounds. As quickly as the hive was opened, it was covered again with a thud. After gathering their senses, wails of distress broke out from hive members as Honey and the doctor bees beheld the young queen beside her new egg. However, their concern was drowned out by the disapproving yowls from drones who had noticed the queen's tiny crew of workers. Even the queen herself, while pretty and sleek, was smaller than they were used to.

"Surely this can't be your daughter? Lilac, what is going on?" Buzzz called. "Just look at the size of her companions!"

"Oh, it's her alright! Just… malnourished." Lilac was swiftly carried to the box's side, so she could greet her future successor. "Welcome Royal! Welcome to my lovely hive! You have so much to learn, my child, but I know you'll do well here. You'll be coming straight to my palace room with me, and you will be versed on the way we do things. You need to know so that you can lead with power." Lilac rambled, giving no space for Royal to interject. She stared at Royal, her eyes burning with maniacal ambition. "Rose, Tulip, Petal, Daisy, Lela, Marigold, Orchid, Pollen, and Honey! Chew through the candy at the box's entrance at once!" Lilac ordered. "No one is to harm Royal. As for her egg…"

"Please, I'd like to keep it in my care!" Royal blurted out, gripping her egg closely. She shivered, blinking as her eyes adjusted to the darkness of the hive.

"Well, whatever." Lilac brushed it off, not seeming to really care.. It was just one egg of the thousands to come.

"Thanks. She's my first… uh, new hive's… egg." Royal couldn't help but stammer. She had hardly known her mother, but it was odd to be here again. It felt like a bad dream. Peering through the mesh, she could finally see Lilac's face. *That's my mom.* She was surprised by how unchanged she appeared, with very few deep lines or wrinkles. Besides her graying fur and her demands to be carried everywhere, no one would be able to tell she was soon to retire. Glancing around the hive that took shape before her, Royal shuddered. She felt small in this open space which was flooded with hybrid, oversized bees. Eyes peered at her and her friends from every direction, burning with thousands of thoughts and emotions. The gathering was overwhelming.

"You'll need to learn how to speak if you intend to become queen of this hive, Royal. Hive Honey Quest is of great importance, and must be transitioned into the right hands." Lilac let out a swift breath, scanning Royal in length.

Royal swallowed hard, attempting to find her bearings. *I need to proceed carefully and wisely.* "Of course. Excuse me, I'm just a bit jumbled from our journey. I wish to know more about the hive, and your drones."

"Oh dear! You must be anxious to meet your prince! He is charming, and will lead beside you with strength!"

Royal froze. "Prince?" she buzzed, faint with shock. This was new. "I don't believe... prince?"

"Now Royal, do you have some sort of problem with that?" Lilac retorted. "This new system has served the hive very well, keeping things in good order. The drones work hard to protect the hive and ensure success. It is a system I have no intention of abolishing. Your soon-to-be king will be the head of the drones, and our hive is unstoppable with their strength. You would do well to come to terms with the idea quickly." She eyed Royal with disdain. "He is already chosen."

Royal knew that this system was probably not her mother's idea. It had to have been Buzzz. Her eyes flashed to the large drone at her mother's side. *Something he would do, to gain power, status, and control in the hive. Lilac is his puppet.* The large drone returned her stare with confidence. She had also known Buzzz briefly before her departure, but he wasn't a "King". He was a leader. He probably had used romance in order to gain more control over the hive. *I will have to be even more careful now, since drones openly carry such leadership here. The hive won't question them, and they are free to wreak havoc as they please without being discovered. This is going to be worse than I had imagined.*

"Royal is looking a bit pale; perhaps Honey should have a look at her." Buzzz hadn't broken eye contact.

"I have my own capable nurse bee, thank you," Royal responded a bit too curtly. She tried to conceal her distaste, but her efforts weren't very effective. That moment, one of Lilac's candy crew interrupted their tense exchange.

"Hey Buzzz, we've chewed through the candy-coated entrance," Orchid licked candy dust from her lips, pleased. She seemed to be the leader of the crew. "Can you come take a look?"

Buzzz glared at Royal once more, his eyes sparkling for a moment with unmasked hatred. Then he broke eye contact as he left to check over their work. Royal relaxed a bit as he departed, letting out a small sigh. *It won't be easy to be embraced here.* She looked down at her egg. *Much less my daughters. This is no place for bees like us. Still, we are here. How will we live?* She glanced at her friends. *If I didn't have them, I'd be lost. I must protect them at all costs.* Royal's uneasy thoughts were soon interrupted by Lilac's hot, menacing words.

"What do you think you are doing?" She challenged harshly. "That is my King! You will not disrespect him. Do you think you're already queen? Watch yourself!" And with that, Lilac signaled to be carried off toward the edge of the crowd.

Royal blinked, taken aback by the Queen's intensity. *It doesn't take much to "disrespect" Buzzz.* Her mind was racing. She sighed, aware that the path laid before her was full of trials. She shared a concerned smile with her friends. "Be safe, my daughters. I suspect there's a lot they want to teach me, even tonight." She sighed as her crew began filing out of the box.

Love smiled back. "We'll be okay, as long as we can be together."

# Chapter 3: Nearly Death

It was getting dark outside, and the last patrols had returned to the hive. Royal was being led to her night cell after a long afternoon of orientation in the throne room with Lilac and Buzzz. Things had been a bit tense between them, but she had learned a lot about the workings of the hive. In fact, her brain swirled with bits of disjointed information that had yet to be processed and organized. She had so many questions and gaps to fill, but her brain couldn't handle any more today. Royal was escorted by Pollen, a worker bee who seemed humble and honest. They had been casually chatting and Royal really enjoyed her. She was the kind of bee Royal hadn't expected to encounter at Hive Honey Quest.

"You are the first decent bee I've met around here!" Royal didn't hesitate to express her gratitude. She peered at the worker with curiosity. *I wonder if she knows of Lighthive. But no... that's far too dangerous to ask.*

Pollen dipped her head respectfully in response and said, "I am happy to be of service, Lady Royal." She then pointed an antenna to an open cell they had approached. Royal gawked at the spacious room before her. It was unlike any accommodations she had ever seen before. In each corner there were beautiful golden honeylamps, illuminating the space with a warm glow. In the center sat a luxurious pollen-stuffed bed, and overall, the room was gorgeous.

"Woah... thank you! This is amazing!" Royal was breath taken.

"You are very welcome! This is our best room. If you need anything, please don't hesitate to ask. I stay in the cell to the right," Pollen exclaimed cheerily.

"Sure Pollen. But... one more thing." Royal hesitated as the worker waited patiently. The queen thought of the loyalty and moral fiber of her children at home as she stared uncomfortably at the ground. Royal was deeply troubled, knowing she would have to conceal her faith from most for the time being, if she wanted to become queen. But with Pollen, she felt safe. Maybe she could help Royal further understand where things stood in the hive.

"Do you... perhaps, have you heard of... Lighthive?" Royal spoke with caution. She wasn't completely sure how touchy the subject would be. *Perhaps it isn't as taboo as I think?*

Pollen's eyes stretched wide. "My goodness, it has been forever since that has been spoken of here!" She eyed Royal with an unreadable expression for a while. "...Yes, I have. But... you must know that any bee who mentions it after a warning is sentenced... to death. You must be careful."

Royal's heart skipped a beat. "...death..." *What has this hive come to?* She had suspected that caution would be necessary in the hive, but had not understood the extent of its downfall. Absolutely no freedom remained for the worker bees. Pollen was searching Royal's troubled eyes.

"Do you follow the aforementioned?" Pollen questioned. After a few moments scanning the room, her eyes came back to meet Royal's. Her voice was low. "You are not alone in that. While quietly, there are a few here who still believe, though most have been snuffed out. Those still alive have resorted to secrecy, but are still loyal. If anything, their faith has been suppressed to a lower level of expression. They still hold on to hope though."

Royal shook her head. "I had no idea it had come to this. Things have changed for the worse since I was last here. It is even more important that my girls and I don't mention..." Royal's voice trailed off. Royal dreaded the fate they would face if they were overheard. "To what degree are we spied on in the hive? I expect there are patrols."

"Yes. You would be wise to watch your back at all times." Pollen's face looked stern. Just then, startling the two insects, two patrol drones barged around the corner at the end of the hall in their direction. Royal held her breath, trying to conjure up anything to avoid suspicion. However, she was not used to this secrecy, and was not very smooth.

"Have you ever seen such a radiant glow? I'm certain you will be very comfortable here." Pollen's expression changed like lightning, and she seemed unphased. Royal was grateful for her swiftness. Then it occurred to her that she must be quite used to this occurring.

"...Oh, yes! I am quite pleased! And that cushion... it looks so soft!" Royal joined in.

"How long does it take for a deer fly to complete a single task? What are you two blabbering about anyway?" Royal analyzed the drone who spoke, noticing that his only ornament was a honey crystal on the tip of his right antenna.

"Yeah, y'all are acting like sick sloths! Or... a dumb dandelion! Or..."

"Shut up Spade!" The first drone spat. He appeared exasperated by his partner's level of cognitive function. Spade did not appear to be very bright, but this other drone had a dangerous look about him. "Come on ya stinkin' birds! In the time you've been dawdling, your friends have been seized. They are about to meet their destruction!"

Royal froze. The blood rushed through her veins and her stance was rigid with anger. "My friends! Where are they?" She spoke in a commanding tone. *How could I have forgotten?* She was ashamed for having left her loyal crew behind somewhere in the hive while she was training. *I should have insisted they stay with me at all times. I KNOW it's not safe for them here!*

"They are lined up for execution." The first drone sneered. "Us drones don't find them fit to work here. They are sickly and small compared to our sisters. And seeing as you have no authority yet..."

"No!" Royal gasped. Her soul was a leaf in Flowerwilt, shriveling and brown. The authoritative countenance she'd worn melted away into devastation, before she shouted again. "Bring me to them!"

"Come and see, if you wish. There is no turning back now." Spade scoffed. Royal forced herself to move even though it felt like all of her muscles were all spasming painfully. Pollen stayed behind, a look of masked fear in her eyes. Royal followed the two evil drones through hallways that seemed to go forever. Time felt warped, and it seemed like hours before they arrived at the scene. The drones led her to an odd, wide room with a low ceiling. It was dimly lit and buzzing with jeers and exclamations. In the center of the crowd, largely consisting of drones, there was a precarious cave of dry leaves assembled together. Spade jeered. "They'll burn alive in that cave!"

Royal's heart seemed to stop as she glimpsed her five friends huddled together in the cave. They appeared bound, and they trembled with fear. Not one looked up. In the center of the huddle was Nectar, Royal's little nurse bee. She simply could not imagine existing here without her daughters. "No! How can you do this!" Her voice was faint and shrill. Terror cemented her to the ground, and she could not seem to move a muscle. She watched, helplessly frozen, as five workers approached the cave, yielding birch shard torches. It was all happening so fast. They were just an inch away when suddenly, a booming voice put a stop to the proceedings.

"I order you to stop this at once!" Buzzz's authoritative voice echoed through the chamber, and the torch bearers halted abruptly. Royal gasped, still unable to move or speak. "You there, in the cave! Come out!"

Royal flinched when her friends' petrified faces came into the light. Why had Buzzz stopped this? He certainly didn't think she would grow to trust him? Had he set all of this up? When Royal's friends noticed her, they cried out at once.

"Royal, save us!" It was Faith, the loyal bee who always persevered and had a special dedication to Lighthive. Another desperate bee cried out.

"Help us Royal!" It was Peace, who was always concerned about the justice and well-being of her friends. The others kept silent. Trust, who was the most considerate and reliable, returned Royal's gaze with complete belief that all would be well. Love, who was the most encouraging and constant of the group, looked as if a terrible spell had entranced her senses. And of course, Nectar. *My little nurse bee. She always cares for her friends and never lets them down.* Royal realized just how close she had come to losing the friends she held most dear forever. Her world was shaken. Suddenly, Buzzz's smooth voice jolted Royal from her trance.

"All of you, follow me. Royal, you too."

# Chapter 4: The Prophecy and the Egg

Buzzz led Royal and her daughters through the halls. He was moving almost mechanically with awkwardness, and the look on his face was odd. "So, I see that my disobedient subjects nearly burned you alive," He buzzed, almost as if he were quoting memorized lines.

"Yes Buzzz. Your disobedient bees nearly burned us alive," Peace mimicked hotly, not worrying about respecting the king. "And we've done nothing wrong! Is there no justice in this hive?"

Next to Peace, Trust looked strangely content. "I knew we'd be alright," she almost whispered.

"I just don't get how your bees are so mean and heartless!" Love burst out sobbing. Faith nodded with a fierce expression. The whole lot looked ruffled, and some, very troubled. Royal turned to Nectar, wanting to hear her sweet voice. The nurse bee was stirring as she recovered from the shock of the experience. She became more focused, and her eyes narrowed as she studied Buzzz's body language suspiciously.

"If you think this has earned our trust, Buzzz, you are mistaken." As Nectar began to speak, a growing light like the sun seemed to glint brilliantly in her eyes. She chanted, " '*There will never be peace with evil in the hive. But when it's purged, love and peace will thrive. All will trust all, and faith will forever flow. This is the prophecy of Lighthive.*' " She never broke eye contact with the drone.

Buzzz gasped, suddenly enraged. He lost his composure and spat, "You shall never speak of your religion here! The name you mentioned is strictly forbidden!" His eyes were hot flames burning into them. Looking around, he made a great effort to control his countenance.

Nectar was not surprised, and brushed him off, almost unphased. "Anyway, Royal," she added warmly, "here is your egg. I was told that her name must be Hope, by my... my 'religion.'" It wasn't uncommon for Nectar, and nurse bees in general, to have a special connection to Lighthive. Sometimes names were given through them for the offspring of the hive.

Royal beheld her beautiful egg. *Hope,* she thought. *Yes. May you be a glimmer of hope for the hive and the bees in it. May you be the hope to fulfill the prophecy of Lighthive.* Back in her old hive, names often held power. Many bees embodied their names in character. She had a strong feeling that it would be the same with Hope. For once, her fear began to melt away, and her eyes shined as she studied the egg.

Buzzz shot Nectar a warning glance. "Do not think you aren't under the same rules as everyone else here. If I hear *anything*," he warned harshly, "your fate will be death." Buzzz paused, and composed himself. He smiled at the company with forced pleasantry. "But you won't be killed without earning the punishment, of course. Consider yourselves... under my protection." And with that, he flew off, seemingly confident in himself.

Trust peered skeptically down the hallway as Buzzz disappeared around the corner. "What a bad actor. Does he think he's been endearing, or that we will now feel safe in his "care"? I may trust many bees, but I will *never* trust *him*!" Peace shivered next to her, and tension hung in the air.

"What happened? I thought I was going to lose you!" Royal had tears in her eyes as she grabbed them all in a group hug.

Nectar spoke up. "When you went for training, we were just hanging around, trying to be casual. You know that foreign hives don't always take kindly to newcomers. We were laying low when a worker came up to us. We never got her name." Nectar paused. "She told us she'd bring us to our quarters so we could rest after our journey, but it all went south fast. In the halls, a group of drones intercepted us and tied us up. We couldn't defend against them. Then, they brought us to that room."

"We were held there for what felt like a few hours. My life flashed before my eyes," Love added. "I have a feeling these drones are capable of serious evil. They just... spat at us, and berated us... until it was time..." Love's eyes welled with hot tears. "As if they were enjoying themselves!" Nectar touched her sister's wing to comfort her.

"We are okay. But Royal," Faith began, "we'd be wise to remember what these drones are capable of. It's even worse than you had known. I believe the bees of this hive are given no choice but to comply with their demands. If not, they'll be cut down."

Peace shuddered, and added, "Living in harmony here is impossible."

Royal sighed. "I am just so glad you are okay. How can I keep you safe?" Her body trembled with the adrenaline it had created, and she still hadn't recovered. She looked down at her egg. "Thank you for looking after Hope." She paused, when her eyes suddenly grew wide. "She must be starving! We should go to my room immediately so I can feed her some formula!" Royal's crew of friends nodded in agreement, wary after their near-catastrophe.

The crew trudged through the unfamiliar hallways silently. They took the time to process what had just happened, and what they had learned about their new home. While still deeply troubled, they had the chance to physically recover from the incident by the time they reached Royal's cell. At the door of her room, they saw Daisy, one of the bees who helped free them from the wooden box. She was carrying a pot of nectar and a small bowl of pollen into Royal's room; This was exactly what Royal needed. As Daisy set the meal down and turned around, she jumped in surprise to see the crowd of bees watching her from the doorway.

"We're sorry," Love interjected truthfully. "We just got here."

"Don't you know it is unkind to beevesdrop? I finish my job just to see a feast-full of eyes spying on me! Oh, not even a maid bee gets her privacy!" Daisy turned and stormed down the hall in a huff.

"Nothing like a little warmth and friendliness..." Love muttered, taken aback.

"It's okay," Trust comforted her. "Everyone is on edge here. Perhaps she's had a rough day. Isn't there good in everybee?" Love was easily reassured.

Royal had already made her way into her beautiful cell to prepare food for her egg, and her friends waited patiently outside.. After making a ball of pollen and nectar for her, she set the egg on her cushion, went to the door on the right of her's, and knocked.

"Come in!" Pollen answered her. "Royal! Are your daughters okay?" It looked as if Pollen had been afraid the whole time Royal was gone.

"Yes..." Royal still could hardly process the gravity of what had almost taken place. Her mind was racing in every direction. She took a long, deep breath. "Yes. They are all okay! Thank Lighthi..." She quickly lowered her voice. Looking up at Pollen's hopeful face, she added. "I just need an empty comb for Hope."

"Hope? I love the name. I have one in that closet over there. I had it made right after you said you wanted to look after her yourself. It was just delivered to my cell today."

"Thank you!" Royal inspected the sturdy wax cell. "It'll be perfect." Normally eggs were tended by caretakers in a designated section of nursery comb in the hive. Royal, however, had no plans of letting Hope leave her sight again. "Also, Pollen, do you know of any cells nearby for my five friends? They need a safe place to stay."

"Yes, actually. There is a lavish four-bee room on the left of yours. Perhaps you can fit one friend in your room with you?"

"Definitely..." Royal pictured all of the open space she had in her cell, "as long as you have an extra cushion!"

"I've got you covered!" Suddenly Pollen looked rushed. "You should probably go. The drones have been watching me more closely lately, and it's near nightfall. They'll be expecting you to retire to your cell. Here's that cushion. Now, go get some rest."

"Yes, goodnight!" Royal hurried out to her friends, handing Nectar the cushion. "You may share my room with me. Love, Trust, Peace, and Faith, you'll stay in that room there." She pointed toward the door to the left of hers. "It has four beds, for four friends." She smiled warmly at them. "Please, don't go anywhere tomorrow before checking in." Her daughters nodded with excitement and entered their room. Royal could hear their gasps of awe as they took in its luxuries, and it made her smile. *I'm so glad they are still here.* She and Nectar exchanged a warm glance before also retiring to their room. Before long, they had arranged a corner for Nectar, and had tucked Hope safely into the comb with the pollen and nectar ball.

"Hope will likely hatch tomorrow. She will be a larva for about a week, and we will feed her the proper solutions. Then, we will cap her comb with wax, and in a week or two, she will emerge, ready to serve." Nectar explained.

"Wow, I have always been a bit removed from the process. It is so fascinating, and so specific!" Royal gazed lovingly at her egg. Looking up at Nectar solemnly, she added, "I thought I'd lost you today. Thank Lighthive you are still here, my dear friend. I'm not sure if I could navigate my situation without your help."

Nectar sighed. She gave Royal a long hug. "Thank Lighthive." She gave a weak smile, clearly deflated and exhausted from the day. "I think some rest will do us both very well." The two bees situated themselves onto their cushions and said goodnight, though it took some time for them to wind down.

Royal contemplated before drifting off. For the next few weeks, she would continue to train, learn how this hive is run, and help Nectar look after Hope. She would get to meet her new daughter soon. And eventually, she'd become queen. Royal didn't suspect her mother would be passing just yet. *Perhaps in a month or two?* She wasn't sure what the future looked like for her and her friends. *But I revel in the joy I have now. I am truly a blessed bee, to have my friends here, and hope within my grasp.* Royal eventually allowed her mind and body to slow down, and huge waves of exhaustion began to crash over her. Soon enough, she gave in and drifted off to sleep.

# Chapter 5: Hope is Born

*Few Weeks Later~*

~A Royal felt herself inevitably sinking into a sticky, golden sea. "Help!" She cried out, to no avail. She looked up just before her head was ruthlessly swallowed up, and she caught a glimpse of Buzzz, who stood there staring down at her. A satisfied, evil grin resided on his face. Royal panicked as she began gulping honey instead of air... with a gasp, she squeezed her eyes, forcing them open. She found herself safely sprawled in her pollen-stuffed bed. Panting, Royal scanned the room as her head cleared. Both Nectar and Hope were sleeping soundly. It was about 7:00 AM, time to rise. Royal was still shaking from her nightmare. *It was just a dream... right?*

Royal looked at Hope beside her, searching for a distraction. Hope was due very soon! She eyed the sealed comb. She could see Hope's golden-lit shape through the wax. She looked more and more like a bee every day. Then, as if on cue, there started to be movement in the comb. Royal gasped. *Is it time?*

"Nectar, Nectar, wake up." Royal gently prodded her nurse bee awake.

Nectar yawned, peering at her beloved queen behind squinted, sleepy eyes. "I had a dream..."

"I did too!" Royal interrupted, speaking louder this time. "We can speak on it later. But first, something more urgent! Do you think Hope could be due? I see her moving about in her comb!"

Nectar's eyes widened. She scanned the comb closely. The whole thing began to wiggle. "Yes! I am going to wake the others quickly!" Nectar rushed out of the cell.

Royal moved closer to Hope, amused as the comb shook. *May you bring hope to fulfill the prophecy of Lighthive! Does Lighthive approve of her name?* Royal knew that Nectar had received the name from Lighthive itself, but she still needed the ceremonial words to be spoken. A wave of peace and assurance told her *yes. Thank you Lighthive.*

Just then, Royal's other daughters burst into the room. "Is she okay?" Love asked. It was clear that none of them besides Nectar had cared for baby bees before. "I wouldn't want anything to happen to her."

Nectar reassured Love. "Don't worry. This is perfectly normal. We all came into this world the same way."

Faith lowered herself to peer at the comb. "Remember the prophecy?" she buzzed with excitement, throwing a sideways glance at Nectar. "Will she bring the hope that we need?" Royal smiled, hopeful.

"Look, she's moving a lot!" Peace gasped.

The bees looked on as the wax seal began to give way. Nectar was close by assisting Hope as she became more visible. After a struggle, Hope's head emerged from the comb with a pop. Nectar leaned the comb against the cushion and helped Hope wiggle the rest of the way out. Royal was fascinated to see that she was fully formed and ready to serve, just as Nectar had explained.

"Hope," Royal recited the ceremonial words, "Do you promise to work your hardest, and to serve your queen even if it costs you your life?"

Hope looked up excitedly. "*Yyesss,*" she muttered, "I do!"

"THE QUEEN IS DEAD!" Buzzz called. Shocked gasps and mutters echoed in the landing grounds, spreading like wildfire around the drone. "She was found in the throne room this morning... and she had passed." Buzzz forced a look of mourning. "Where is Royal? She will be needed today. There are ceremonies to take place."

"She is in her cell!" Spade, the less intelligent drone, responded.

"Fetch her at this very instant, and take Clubb with you." Clubb stepped forward, adorned with the usual singular ornament on his antenna.

"Yes sir!" Spade buzzed dramatically as Clubb rolled his eyes.

ROYAL WAS GAZING PLEASANTLY into Hope's eyes, soaking in the moment, when she heard a familiar voice approaching through the hall.

"How late does a stinkin' deer fly sleep?" It was Clubb, followed by Spade. "The queen is dead. Did you not hear?"

Royal and her companions gasped. Hope's questioning eyes flashed. "I thought... aren't *you* the queen?"

Royal sighed. "Nectar, please stay here with Hope. Tell her... everything. Everything she needs to know. I will not be able to. The queen is dead, and I am to be crowned on this very day. Today brings change." Royal turned solemnly to her daughters. "If you four wish to attend, you may." It had been a few weeks since their arrival, and the hive had generally accepted the workers. They could now wander about and do a bee's work, mostly unbothered. Turning to Hope, Royal whispered, "I'll be back to spend time with you soon."

"Hurry up, or we're comin' in!" Clubb was growing impatient.

"We are coming!" Peace rolled her eyes.

Before Royal left the room, Nectar grabbed her arm. She leaned forward and whispered into Royal's ear. "I had a dream..." That was all she said.

Royal walked with the drones, pondering her own horrible dream. *I wonder if Nectar's was similar, or something completely different. What does it mean? Does Buzzz intend to harm me?* She was thoughtful. *No matter, it will have to wait until later. Today will be eventful.* Royal blankly followed the two drones toward the main entrance. A part of her was excited to finally resume queenly activities. However, she wished it weren't here. Every hive had different customs, so she didn't exactly know what to expect. She just hoped that somehow she could change this hive for the better. Observing the sun peeking into the hive's entrance, Royal guessed that the first hiveline and flower patrols of the day would be returning shortly. Right then, her thoughts were interrupted by Buzzz's mocking voice.

"Hello, Royal. What kept you in your cell for so long?" Buzzz bowed rigidly. "The queen has passed. Now that she is gone, it is time for you to meet your mate and take leadership." There was a veiled hint of accomplishment in his voice. *Shouldn't he be the most sorrowful?* Royal thought bitterly. *No, I'm pretty sure he had no love in him. Just a hunger for power. But I won't be so easily controlled, now will I?* She did not respond with more than a glance. Taking a breath, she stood tall, ready to take on this day.

# Chapter 6: The Daydream

"Sting? Step forward," Buzzz ordered as a large drone parted through the crowd, breaking into the inner circle. Royal had seen her friends being forced out to the edges, and she was now completely surrounded by drones. She was too bombarded to see much more. This part of her crowning had been filling her with the most trepidation over the weeks as she anticipated it. Sighing, she looked up at Sting who now stood before her. He was a handsome and fit young drone, just shorter than Buzzz. His furry coat was sparkling with tiny honey crystals, and he was wearing a crown of woven grass which bore an intricate and fascinating design. Unexpectedly, Royal's breath caught in her chest at the sight of him.

"I am Sting." Royal took note of his unusually soft and gentle tone. "I am proud to become your king. I will serve you, and catch you when you fall. I will offer a hand when you stumble. I will be here when you need help and support. I will lead and train the drones of our hive with pride."

Royal gazed into his eyes intently. *Can he actually be okay? ...No... how could he be, raised as a drone in this hive?* Royal's mind swirled with questions as Sting's gaze met hers unwaveringly. *Was he not mentored by Buzzz? Surely he is a pawn for the tyrant's plans... Or perhaps, there is still good in the heart of this hive, amidst the evil?* Buzzz's loud announcement paused Royal's thoughts.

"Royal, do you accept Sting as your mate and King?"

Royal slowly nodded, much to her own surprise. She felt an odd peace about this, though she had previously dreaded this moment the most. "Y...yes... I do."

"Sting, do you accept your position, and promise to aid the queen and protect the hive, even if it ends in your death?"

Sting agreed quickly with a word, "Yes," then added a bit awkwardly, "I do." He looked over at Buzzz subtly, as if to ask for his approval.

Buzzz nodded with satisfaction. "And so it is. Royal is our Queen, and Sting our king!" He looked so at ease, it troubled Royal. "Tonight, Royal shall move into her new quarters, the throne room. Tomorrow at sundown, a flight ceremony will take place," Buzzz informed while laying a pretty vine crown atop Royal's head, "preceded by the beedances and patrols. Everyone who is able must join in." The crowd cheered with excitement.

Not sure how to feel, Royal glanced as Buzzz's eyes. Before she could think, she began to slip into a daydream. His eyes reflected gold, resembling pools of honey, deep and threatening to drown her. She watched in horror as her mother, Lilac, fell into the honey, flailing her arms as she was sucked under. She heard Nectar's whisper echoing "*I had a dreammm...*" *Nectar must have found a way to share her dream.* It was there and gone so fast, it was dizzying. Remembering her own dream, Royal gasped. She had connected the dots. She and Nectar had been given pieces of the puzzle, and now it was clear. She blinked her eyes to restore her vision, shaking her head. Buzzz was looking down on her with a smirk of satisfaction plastered on his face. *Buzzz... is a murderer. He killed Lilac!*

"SO, MY MOM LAID ME in that tiny box?"

"Yes, and she has watched you like a hawk ever since!" Nectar answered Hope. Royal had told Nectar to tell her *everything*. So, she was doing her best. "When we arrived here, she kept you with her, right at her bedside, and helped care for you herself."

"Really?" Hope looked up, wide-eyed. Usually eggs were kept in a nursery comb and cared for by a team of workers. "Didn't you say we are in a bad place? I need to know, how can I serve my mother?"

Nectar's face turned grave. "Hope, we have been transported into a very twisted hive. Things are not as they should be. Drones are adorned with honey, pollen, and beeswax ornaments as objects of vanity. They are large and strong, and live many times longer than they should. Here, the drones are in control. They are ruthless punishers if you step out of line. Be careful, dear. Doing the right thing is dangerous here." Hope opened her mouth to speak, but Nectar signaled for her to wait. "Hope, your name was given to me by Lighthive. Lighthive is all things good and right, and the drones here will not allow mention of it. The light guides our steps, and names are given for a reason. We believe Lighthive has a special purpose for you... In some way, you are to help us break free of the tyranny that now stands. You are young, yes, but know that you are important."

Hope was silent as the weight of Nectar's words sank in. *Important...* It was overwhelming to think that she, as young and naive as she was, would play an important role in all of this somehow. *Talk about being born into struggle...* Something about all of this rang true within her, but it was a heavy burden to carry. *How can I live up to these expectations?*

Interrupting her thoughts, Royal called out excitedly from the doorway. "Hope? I'm back. I don't have much time today, but wanted to drop in. How are you?" She peered at her daughter with care.

"I'm... just trying to soak it all in. I'm happy to see you." She gave her mom a warm hug.

Royal smiled. "You must be tired and overwhelmed. Why don't you and the girls take a break? How would you like to pollinate some flowers? You could beat the rush and get the most sweet, plentiful nectar."

Hope's eyes sparkled. "YES! I can't wait to taste fresh nectar!" She did a little spin, glad to take a breath and do something lighthearted.

"Then let's go," Peace buzzed, "this place is always so noisy!"

Hope quickly forgot about the trouble within the hive. She squinted at the bright rays of light that crept through the main entrance. This would be her first time outside, and she was ecstatic! Wide-eyed, Hope began to take it all in as they passed through the opening. Nature was beautiful. The air smelled fresh and bright. While everything she took in was new, it also felt so natural, as if she'd seen it before.

Love began to lead the way through a vast forest and gallant meadow until they reached a flower patch that resided a distance from the hive. Faith demonstrated how to extract nectar, though Hope's instincts were keen. She eagerly awaited her turn, overwhelmed with joy and a sense of discovery.

"It's so sweet!" Hope was amazed. "And... there is such abundance!" The bees went to work, and all were very focused on the task at hand. Neither of them had tasted fresh nectar in days, and they were long overdue. Distracted by their task, a peculiar dark cloud began to roll into a corner of the sky, allowing the sun to still shine brilliantly despite its presence. Without warning, giant raindrops began to fall lazily from the sky. They were so massive, they were hard to dodge.

"Oh... no!" Trust gasped after the spray of a raindrop showered her head and she faltered in the air.

"We have to find shelter, *immediately*." Love kicked right into action. "We can't make it home in this-we are out too far." Pausing, she glanced at Hope with fearful eyes. "Heavy rainfall can mean freezing or drowning, as well as battering."

The bees shuddered as they scanned the area for shelter. Before long, Peace exclaimed, "This way!" Trusting, the bees followed her and her keen eyes to a large shelterleaf close to the ground. They flew cautiously toward the leaf, dodging raindrops as they approached. It was the only one of its kind nearby, and was just big enough to cover the whole company. They took cover just in time before the rain began falling harder.

"We are very lucky... there isn't much to protect us in an open field. It could easily have been our deaths." Love looked sober as she spoke, the weight of her tone apparent. "We must huddle to stay warm. Warmth is essential to our survival."

Hope was again left to her brooding thoughts. What if she and her friends died? *They believe I am an essential part of fulfilling a prophecy.* She remembered the words Nectar had recited, bubbling with frustration at them. She had only been hatched for a minute before the weight of the world was on her shoulders. Like the beautiful, sunny day, she arrived with optimism and excitement. But without warning or invitation, things shifted so fast. This pressure was unexpected, unwanted, and unrelenting, just like the raindrops pelting upon the shelterleaf. *Perhaps it will drip off... or the rainfall will end. Soon enough it will be forgotten. I am too young for this burden, and I am not ready!* She hid her tears as they descended. *I do not want this!*

# Chapter 7: The Daughters Return

Royal had been lost in thought. *What did Buzzz hope to gain in killing his queen? Or was he just sick of her? Nothing will stop him from doing the same to me if he so pleases. He will unapologetically do whatever he wants in order to increase his power.* Royal shuddered. Orchid's words snapped her back to reality.

"Here is the beautiful throne where you will lay your eggs," Orchid explained. Royal had spent some time with this highly-ranked bee. She was one of the bees who helped her and her daughters out of the wooden box. She seemed to be in charge of a lot.

"Your queen does not lay eggs directly into the nursery comb?" Royal was taking in the hive's oddities. "Hm. Is there a cell nearby for my friends?" She didn't want to be alone here. At least the close company of her friends would ease her mind.

"The only cells nearby are for higher ranked bees like me," she paused, "and for the drones."

Royal's stomach lurched when she saw two single-bee cells in the far corner of the room. Hanging limply from each doorknob were signs reading "King Sting" and "Buzzz". The fancy print did nothing to ease Royal's alarm. *What kind of leadership does Buzzz still think he has?* "I need to have my friends nearby," Royal demanded through clenched teeth. After weeks of staying calm, learning, and training, she was bubbling over, exasperated.

"Not here!" Orchid snapped, nearly shouting. Her voice trailed off weakly. "Not here... not here..." Royal tried to read her changing expression. She thought she could detect fear in Orchid's veiled eyes, when it suddenly changed back to a defensive, furious glare. "Why? Can't you fare without them? You *are* the queen!"

Royal was frustrated and puzzled. Why did everybee act so strange? Why was their behavior so unnatural and confusing? Gathering herself, she blurted out. "What is going on here, and why won't anyone be real with me? I must know, Orchid. Explain! What's going on?" She overflowed with questions she had bottled inside. "Aren't *I* the queen? Don't *I* make the orders? Why is everybee unreceptive to my questions? Help me out here!" Royal wiped away a hot, angry tear.

After a moment's pause, Orchid's expression softened just slightly. She responded, a trace of sympathy in her guarded voice. "I... I know how it is, Royal." She scanned the room cautiously. "But... we are always being watched. There's no way out, Royal, no escape. We just have to trust that we will pull through." She sighed. "I'll try my best to bring your friends near."

Royal sighed. Orchid's words were heavy. For a moment, she too was overtaken with defeat. Then, something dawned on her. She wasn't alone! *How many other bees feel this way? Would there be enough? Enough to... rebel?*

LOVE LET OUT A LONG, relieved sigh as the five shivering bees reached the warmth of Hive Honey Quest's entrance. The downpour had been brief, but tumultuous, and their shelter held up just long enough to protect them. However, the whole ordeal had left them tired and skittish. They were eager to bring their core temperatures back up. Hope still brooded in her thoughts, but she was doing her best to ignore them.

"I knew we would make it... as long as we stuck together," Faith muttered. Love, Peace, and Trust nodded in agreement. The bees stumbled in as the hive guards nodded to let them pass.

"We must find Nectar and Royal," Trust gasped, realizing how late it was getting. The exhausted insects stumbled through halls until they reached their cells, only to find them empty.

"Huh? Where's Nectar, and where is my mom?" Hope asked, frazzled.

"Perhaps mother is where a queen bee belongs. I suppose Nectar would be with her as well. A queen's throne room is usually deep within the hive," Love sighed.

Hope wandered through the two cells, looking for any sign of Royal. "Hey, look! There's a note on mom's bed!" She hastily unfolded the birch page as her sisters gathered around her. Written carefully in yellow with a dandelion petal, the note read:

*Dear my beloved friends,*
*I am off to the throne room. Meet me in the*
*landing grounds at 7:30. Nectar is with*
*Honey, my mother's old nurse bee. I look*
*forward to seeing you all, my friends.*
*Love,*
*Queen Royal*

"Oh, thank goodness! They're both alright," Hope buzzed. Love happily snatched the letter from Hope and read it for herself, the rest of the crew peering over her shoulder. Their faces brightened.

"We can't be late," Trust cried in determination. "It is nearly 7:30 now!" The five eager bees zoomed through the network of hallways leading to the landing grounds. The ordeal took almost all of the energy they had left. When they arrived at the meeting place, it was not a moment too soon.

"Royal?" Peace called hopefully. "Are you here?" Her voice echoed through the large space which was eerily empty. Hope started to worry again. She needed to see her mother. She already had been robbed of the time she may have had with her. Maybe talking to the Queen would help calm her mind and ease her burden.

"Mom?" Hope called in desperation.

"Turn around, young bee." The crew heard a voice behind them, and quickly turned. There, Buzzz himself hovered. "Come along, I'll bring you to Royal."

Suspicion and fear welled up in Hope's thorax. Nectar had described this very drone and his ornaments to her earlier, and had warned her about him. *This is Buzzz, alright.* "Where is my mother?" She demanded. *If he's done something to her...*

"Relax!" Buzzz chuckled in amusement. "Is there a moth stuffed in your throat? Royal was simply unaware of the authority meeting she had to attend at 7:00. She insisted that someone come down here to meet with you guys." He paused, tilting his head. "On that note, where have you been? No one has seen you since sunhigh."

Trust cleared her throat. "I believe you haven't come to dance around unimportant topics."

Buzzz glared suspiciously at Trust. "Indeed. Follow me. Royal has requested to see you right away after the meeting." The group cautiously followed Buzzz to an open room near the back of the hive. It was filled with nutshell chairs lined around a wooden table. Many senior and highly-ranked bees were there, including Royal, who sat on the end beside King Sting. Buzzz gestured to the crew of newcomers. "I found them. Not sure what they've been up to, but they all look terrible."

"SO WE HAVE TO LOOK for other bees that disapprove of the madness here, befriend them, and then eventually form a potential rebellion?" Nectar asked timidly. After an hour of frivolous talk, the she-bees had at last deterred the drone guards, who had appeared bored out of their minds when they left. Finally awarded some privacy, they could get to the point without any unwanted listeners. Moments like these were rare in Hive Honey Quest. Still, they proceeded cautiously in hushed tones.

"Yes. We need to be social insects. Get to know as many bees as possible!" Royal responded in a hushed tone. "I can take care of the drone population, despite my doubts in finding many recruits there. We have to be fast, but cautious; this is beyond dangerous. Here is a list of the job systems this hive has in place. We must cover as many groups as possible."

*Bee Groups:*
*Doctors*
*Maids*
*Nurses*
*Fighters*
*Adventurers*
*Explorers*
*Caretakers*
*Guards*
*Scientists*
*Flower Specialists*
*Enemy Researchers*
*Hive Planners*
*Hive Builders*
*Undertakers*
*Drones*
*Queen(s)*

"Wow..." Love stammered. "There is so much to cover."

"How much time do you suppose we have?" Peace questioned.

Royal paused thoughtfully before proceeding. "Ladies, there is no telling what Buzzz's plans for you or this hive may be. I know it sounds crazy, but we need to work fast." She took a breath. "I think we have two weeks... at most." Royal flinched at their astonished reactions. "I know it sounds impossible. But you must realize, the hive is on edge. Something dangerous is brewing here. If we can, we'll need to strike first. We have to prepare... prepare for war."

# HOPE

"Am *I* meant to fight in a war?" Hope, who hadn't spoken until now, quietly interrupted her mother. They all turned to her with surprised expressions. Hope still believed she was too young to fulfill some prophecy. *This cannot have to do with me. I know so little! It just can't be me...* she thought to herself. Her sisters' faces were filled with mixed emotions. Fear, faith, terror, confidence... it was penetrating. They depended on her. The most prevalent expression was that of hope. *Hope...*

# Chapter 8: First Progresses in Secrecy

"Hello Pollen!" Royal had finally gotten most things in order as the new queen, and she had completed all of the ceremonies. It was nearly time for bed. The setting sun cast long shadows outside, but Royal couldn't be restful. Her daughters had begun recruiting. She also shared that mission, and her intuition told her that Pollen was just the place to start. *She is humble, kind, and exudes a spirit of goodness.* Royal was confident she would join the cause, and become an important member, at that. She had casually made her way toward Pollen's cell in hopes of intercepting her. After an awkward moment of dawdling, Pollen had emerged from the bend in the hallway, and Royal had greeted her.

"Hello Royal!" Pollen responded, pleasantly surprised. "Need something?" She gestured for Royal to join her in her cell. Over the last few weeks, the neighbors had become quite close. With Royal's crowning and relocation, however, it would be difficult to maintain their friendship without suspicion.

Royal began by organizing what to say in her head. This would be the first of many recruitments, and probably the easiest. But, it was difficult to present. "Well, I have a question for you, Pollen." *I trust her enough to go straight to the point.* "Do you believe that our hive, my hive, can be rescued from the evil within?"

Pollen sighed. "If only..."

"But it can!" Royal blurted out. Glancing around, she lowered her voice. "Help me, Pollen. I... am slowly building a rebellion. I think that now is the right moment to challenge Buzzz and all that he stands for." She paused gravely. "There will be war. It is inevitable at this point if we hope to be free. But Lighthive-willing, we will spare this hive of its dreadful burden. We..."

"I'm in." Someone chimed as the door creaked open. Standing there was a drone. It was Thistle. Royal and Pollen were both rigid, aware of their mistake. "I am persistently tormented for being almost normal-weak, they say. I was born ready for a rebellion. If you will fight my half-brother Buzzz and the evil he enforces, then I am more than ready."

Royal let out a sharp breath. "Thank Lighthive you weren't Spade or Clubb!" She saw Thistle flinch at the mention of Lighthive.

"I apologize, Your Majesty. I'm not very accustomed to certain freedoms... yet. Maybe that will change." Thistle spoke slowly, his voice brimmed with hope and conviction. "I understand that it may be hard to trust a drone here. But you should know that I have been yearning to challenge things here for some time. It's simply... impossible to do alone."

"I should just be more careful!" Royal peered worriedly at the door. *After three weeks, I'm still not used to having to watch my back all the time.* Almost on cue, the door swung open with force.

"Hushhh!!! What if I were Buzzz?" Faith whispered solemnly, as she and numerous companions entered the room until it was full. With her was Love, Trust, Peace, Nectar, Orchid, and several others Royal did not recognize. Royal was pleased to see Orchid in the crowd. She looked very uneasy-almost as if she was ready to bolt. But she was here, and that counted for something.

"Royal," Love started, "meet Lily, Marigold, Pea, Blossom, Petal, Mint, Willow, Auburn, and Sage. All are here, aware, and ready to serve our purpose."

Royal nodded warmly at the newcomers, smiling. She counted up in her head. *10 bees besides us so far. That's a start... not bad for day one. Where... is Hope?* Panic welled up in Royal's chest as she felt the absence of her precious daughter. She knew that any of her daughters were at risk of being targeted or hurt, especially when alone. "Wait...

Hope? Where is she?" She scanned the faces of her friends. "Faith? Love? Nectar? Where is Hope?"

Alarm flashed in Nectar's eyes. "You haven't seen her? She went for a breath of fresh air, but that was at least an hour ago. She could be in danger!" The company exchanged nervous glances. They didn't know what would happen if Hope wasn't there as things came together. Would they even have a chance without her?

"We need to find her, and quickly! But we can't act strange." Royal controlled the dread she felt inside and spoke calmly. "Peace, Love, Trust, Faith, and... Pea? You five should patrol the farm looking for any traces of her." Realizing it was night, she added, "Of course you can't go now. Leave at first light tomorrow morning. If she's out there, she'll have to fare for the night."

Pea spoke for the first time. "Yes, Your Highness!" Pea was a pretty young worker with kind eyes. Her voice was light and high, like the sound of a gentle drizzle on the hive roof. "That will work excellently with my schedule." She added, "I presume we need to keep a low profile, so I think we should stick to our normal daily tasks as much as possible."

"Pea makes a good point." Royal nodded in approval. She addressed the recruits, trying to stay collected. "However, you also all have connections in this hive that us newcomers don't have. We need to be recruiting as many bees as possible whenever there is free time. You may have bees in mind who will be receptive to the cause. Start there. It is imperative that we don't blow our cover by speaking to the wrong bees." Speaking to her daughters now, she added, "Would you search the hive for Hope tonight? Try to be casual. Don't search every nook and cranny, just check the halls and main working areas. We need to check that box off before you begin the outside search tomorrow."

Orchid piped up, her voice wavering. "How will we know when it is time to rebel?" She glanced at the door and lowered her voice to a whisper. "We should all be... on the same page. It is hard to imagine assembling possibly thousands of bees with such little time to communicate."

Royal looked at Orchid gravely. "While we have a general time frame, we need to wait for the right moment. I'm afraid I can't be sure when that will be. You should always be on guard, and try to confirm the status of things before starting to fight." She turned to the other recruits. "We may be very outnumbered. We can hope that others will rebel with us when they understand what is happening, but we can't know for certain. That is why it is crucial to recruit as many bees as we possibly can. I believe we need to work fast, because I can sense that our time is running short."

"Royal, drones approaching." Nectar walked in from the doorway. "Remember, we are having a party to celebrate the new Queen." The bees began buzzing excitedly. Royal again marveled at how quickly and easily the hive members could redirect. It was seamless. *It's happening. Before long... we will free this hive!*

PEA SHOOK THE SLEEP from her wings and peeled off her covers. *Knock knock.* She quickly combed her hair and rubbed her eyes. *Knock knock.* "I'm coming," she whispered. She sucked up a mouthful of honey from her beeswax bowl and went briskly to the door.

"I know I'm early. But I think we should be getting an early start," Peace whispered urgently. It was 5:23 AM, about 7 minutes earlier than planned. The rest of the morning search party stood next to her, yawning. They had not seen a trace of Hope in the hive last night, and the sisters were eager to find her. Pea hadn't really met Hope yet, but she was ready to help in any way she could. She was a vibrant and hard-working bee, and had been suffering in silence for quite some time. Sweet Pea had always sought a deeper connection in friendships, but it was hard to come by in a hive controlled by fear. She was ready to break the chains.

"I'm ready!" Pea straightened. "Where do we begin?"

Love pulled out a folded map of the farm and a sharp dandelion petal for tracing a path. "We will start in Shadow Forest. Then we will embark along the Stream of Crashing Waters, check through Alfalfa Field, fly across the Fruitful Farm Road, and skirt the HoneyBandit's Hive. We will check the Gardens there, then continue over the Flower Meadow. We should reach the other forest's edge and the Stream of Quiet Ripples. Unless we find Hope right away, it's going to be a long journey. It will definitely last more than just a day." Love paused. "We need to keep an eye out for anything unusual or dangerous. Keep a close watch for horsefly herds or hornets. We should check under and all over each of the popular pollination spots in our path."

The workers nodded. Trust interjected. "Have we considered the possibility that Hope has left willingly?" Her question was met with shocked expressions.

"Why would she do that?" Love queeried.

"I think we just need to be aware of the possibilities. If she wants to stay hidden, we will not find her. But if she's in trouble and needs our help, we will be there." Trust concluded.

"We should get started," Faith said, attempting to shake Trust's words.

"Yes, let's go." Love and the party flew briskly to the entrance of the hive. The hive guards were asleep-save for one, who eyed them suspiciously before nodding to let them pass.

The morning was dark and cold, but the sun finally started to peak over the horizon to warm the earth. From the start, the bees were solemn and silent, feeling the urgency of the task at hand. They didn't know why, but Hope was important. She was needed. Love had taken the lead, a bit uncertain as she checked the map. "Pea, do you know the farm?"

Pea hesitated. "Yes, I am an adventurer. I know the farm well." She smiled, then added, "However, if Hope has left or has been taken, don't you think she may have gone beyond the farm's boundaries?"

Love looked thoughtful. "Your thought may be true, but I know nothing outside the farm, and neither does she."

"I have been outside the farm boundaries many times. I am one of the bees who makes maps like the one you hold." Pea spoke with pride. "I know of some places of significance that are not far from the farm's edge. There is one place in particular that seems to draw bees in... it's called the Mountain of the Sun. If Hope has gone purposefully, I believe she could be there. And if she was taken, there are friends nearby who may have seen her. I think we would be wise to check there on the way. It is just a bit further north through another small forest."

Peace hummed. "We should patrol the farm first. If we don't find her here, then we should venture further toward this mountain. It sounds fascinating." Love nodded in agreement. Faith and Trust were looking at each other, their eyes alight. Then, all at once, the company realized they had been resting on a sunflower, stationary.

"We should be getting a move on!" Trust exclaimed. Stretching their wings, they took flight. Love gestured for Pea to take the lead. She reluctantly went ahead, not wanting to be disrespectful to Love's leadership. Love waved her arm again to encourage her.

Hours passed. The workers tried to leave no stone unturned, and progress was slow. Still, there was not even a trace of their lost sister. The sun rose and fell, and they were exhausted. As it grew darker, the party reached the Stream of Quiet Ripples. In a few still pools, female damselflies were daintily laying their eggs.

"I wonder what it's like to be a queen," Peace thought aloud dreamily.

"Wouldn't you rather fly freely and pollinate flowers?" Pea speculated, panting.

Peace pondered that for a moment. "Yes, I suppose, but it still sounds so grand. Either way, I'm just happy to have my sisters. I can't imagine life without my family."

Pea's face drooped. "Yeah, family." She slowed down. "Family is a blessing."

"Do you have any family?" Trust buzzed, noticing Pea's countenance had changed. "That is, beyond the usual interrelation of a hive."

"I have a brother." Pea responded after a moment. "Iris. He is such a brilliant drone." She took a long breath. "He's a good drone, but he's eager to please Buzzz and be the best he can be for him. What if he chooses him over me?"

The she-bees were quiet, listening as Pea shared her heart with them.

"He's pretty close friends with Thistle, who favors our way of thinking. Yet, I'm worried that when it comes down to it, I'll have to battle against my own blood. I don't know what I'd do."

Before anyone could respond, a new voice shouted from a little ways off, shattering their moment of comradery. "Awww, can we join your little buzz fest?" Hovering nearby was a herd of horseflies. While they didn't prey on bees, they were no doubt a nuisance, and sometimes a danger to them. More than anything, they were bullies. However, there were stories that claimed they were more dangerous, even feeding on insects like vampires. The crew had no plans to test the waters.

"Flee!" Love cried.

"What," another horsefly called angrily, "I ain't no flea!" The gang began to charge.

*Oh no!* Pea thought. *Fly, Pea, fly!*

# Chapter 9: The Wild Hive

"Fly, fly!" Love cried. "Pea, take the lead! Try to lose them!"

"Pee? What kind of dummy are you to be called *Pee?*" A female horsefly whinied. Pea flew ahead and raced out toward Flower Meadow. The horseflies were in hot, unrelenting pursuit. No matter how much she tried to lose them, it was wide open in the field, and they were too easily spotted. Their pursuers were sharp. Trying to hide wasn't a reliable option either. *We need to change course.* Sweet Pea took a sharp and sudden turn toward the edge of farm territory. They were heading as fast as they could toward the trees of a small forest. *If we're lucky, they might just be watching...* As they approached the wood, the horseflies were still gaining on them. But then something odd happened. She looked back and saw the herd abruptly halt in mid-air. *Could it be?*

A strong, clear voice projected. "Back off, blood-eaters! Shoo!" A scruffy honey bee of very wild and natural appearance came into view from the forest's edge. The herd was terrified and had already turned around. In mere moments, the pursuers slipped out of sight, their loud buzzing fading into the distance. As the horseflies were no longer in sight, the five she-bees turned to their mysterious helper, gasping for air in an attempt to recover from their sprint.

"Greetings!" He smiled confidently. He was a sturdy drone of noble frame and appearance. He wore no ornaments of beeswax or pollen. In his hand was a staff. It was made of a rose thorn embedded in a strong twig, steadied with a grapevine. He looked like a warrior, strong and brave, and was unlike any drone the girls had encountered before. "Company, do not fear. You must be in need of a safe place to rest, and regain your strength!"

Love, Trust, Peace, and Faith glanced at Pea, uneasy. While exhausted, they had no idea who the drone was or where he had come from. They weren't sure if they could trust the stranger.

"I assure you, I mean you no harm." He comforted them.

Pea broke eye contact with the others uncomfortably. "Kind sir, I am not certain if you remember me, but I have been a guest of your people before. I am Sweet Pea."

He tilted his head in sudden recognition. "Ah! A friend! It has been some time, Sweet Pea. Greetings! Pardon me for not recognizing you at once." The drone was smiling widely. "You and your friends are welcome to visit our humble abode." He looked at the others. "Come. My home lies yonder by the birch, in that sturdy, honest oak. Do tell, how are you all feeling? Are there any wounds to be attended to?"

"We're okay..." Trust was staring at the drone quizzically. The sisters had never encountered such a drone, and his very existence stumped them. He spoke with eloquence and unique language as if he had teleported from a hundred years ago. On top of that, he was nothing like any of the drones at Hive Honey Quest, or even the drones in their native hive. "Forgive me, I have never seen a drone like you before."

The stranger laughed. "We aren't common, I suppose." He paused before continuing, composing himself with an air of importance. "In our hive, the drones have duty and honor. We are protectors of the hive, feared far and wide by those who mean to do us harm. But there is no need for you to fear us. Bees are friends! If I may know, where have you flown from, and what is the nature of your journey?"

The company hesitated, but there was nothing to say other than the truth. Peace spoke slowly. "We... are workers of Hive... Honey Quest, about six beelines south of here."

The drone came to a halt, his eyes growing wide. He was quiet for a moment. "A hive we are aware of, for certain." He paused again, his face becoming decisive. "No matter, it is just a place. Not all who dwell there will reflect its ambitions. And the nature of your journey?"

Sweet Pea let out a quick breath. "One of ours has gone missing. A dear friend. We cannot be certain if she was hurt, taken, or if she may have left willingly. Nonetheless, we... we need her." Pea lowered her voice out of habit. "We do not approve of the workings of our hive. Slowly, we are building a resistance. Our friend has an important role in that, and we need all the help we can get, as well as support and friendship. She is greatly missed."

The drone listened thoughtfully. "This is good news. If anyone is to correct the hive's ways, it will start from the inside. To be honest, if you," he gestured toward Pea, "were not leading this party, I would be obligated to keep you all as far from our home as possible. These are dangerous waters to tread in." He faced the others. "But, Sweet Pea has earned our trust and respect, despite us having been unaware of her place of origin. It is always good to see an old friend. You will be welcomed for the night to regain your strength."

The group continued toward the oak, and the workers started to relax a little. "What is your name, sir?" Faith asked.

The drone glanced back at them as they flew. "I am called Sir Taves the Worthy. You can refer to me as Sir Taves. And how shall I refer to you all?"

"I am Faith. This is Love, Trust, and Peace. And, well, you already know Pea."

"It is encouraging to see a group of such decent workers seeking to bring change." Sir Taves smiled. "We have had many run-ins with the folk of Hive Honey Quest. The drones are often terrible to behold. But, we have chosen a life of peace, and have relocated our pollination preferences to a new territory to avoid confrontation. The edge of this wood is where our well-defended territory begins. It just so happens that I was on patrol when I heard the commotion. It seems Lighthive is on your side today."

The company exchanged surprised glances. Their rescuer had spoken of the faith they silently shared. This helped to put them at ease.

Not much further into the small wood, they approached the sturdy oak which housed the wild hive. Its entrance, a large hollow in the trunk, was buzzing with activity. The guards let them in without hesitation, nodding at Sir Taves.

As their eyes adjusted to the low light, the group were gawking in wonder. They had only been accustomed to domesticated hives with the same predictable layout, but this hive was absolutely unique. The bees here had created a beautiful and intricate system. Their comb was plentiful, and was located higher in the trunk where it was well protected. It was independent of any removable frames, and twisted and turned as it pleased, spiraling upwards. The crevice they had built in was not the entire trunk, but a strange pocket in a portion of it. The tree around them was living and strong. This hive would have many years here, without a doubt. The workers took all of it in, awestruck. Sweet Pea was just smiling, happy to return again. *This place is just as fascinating as ever.* Before they knew it, Sir Taves had led them to the top.

They wound through a narrow corridor which led to a grand and spacious opening. Suppressing their gasps, they took in the scene. Thin wood in a few strategic places on the wall allowed just enough sunshine through to dimly light the room. Woven vines and grass constructed divine furniture, and fresh flower petals littered the floor as a bright path to the throne. At the podium, a beautiful queen sat, surrounded by her royal court members on either side. Sir Taves made his way toward the throne without hesitation.

"Sir Taves!" The queen dipped her head in respect, as did the knight. "I see your patrol may have yielded something unexpected. I trust you have screened our guests?" She was a large, mature queen with a honey-smooth voice that radiated with warmth and wisdom. Atop her head sat a small but majestic woven crown with tiny, pink flowers.

"Yes, Your Majesty! Our friend Sweet Pea and her company require a place of rest tonight. They are on an imperative mission that we would be wise to aid." Sir Taves still had his head dipped in respect.

"Explain further, Sweet Pea." The queen gestured at Pea, attentive.

"Your Highness, It brings me great joy to be here again. We were passing by the edge of your forest when we were intercepted by a herd of horseflies. Sir Taves spotted us while on patrol, and he protected us." She paused. "Our company is searching for a dear friend who has gone missing. She is an important piece of our small but growing rebellion. I and my fellow workers have come from Hive Honey Quest, a neighbor to you, which I am certain you know much about."

The queen nodded slowly, her eyes sparkling with interest.

"An opportunity has finally come to challenge the twisted system there. There is a new queen in the hive, who arrived with these workers you see beside me, and she has brought with her a fire for what is right. Slowly, we are recruiting oppressed bees to overthrow our drones' reign. I am one of their recruits, and the others are continuing to build a resistance. We hope to gather enough numbers to stand a chance." Just then, Pea had a brilliant thought. "We ask for lodging tonight, if you'll have us. And if you believe in our cause, we ask of you, a boon."

"You ask for a boon?" The queen tipped her head. "What is it you request?"

Pea dipped her head and proceeded. "The chance of us gathering a big enough army in the little time we have is... unlikely. We may very well be challenging thousands of bees. Not everyone there disagrees with the way things are run." Pea was done dancing around the question. "I know you prioritize peace in this hive. But, if you see our cause as worthy, help us."

The queen was silent, and her eyes didn't break contact. She waited for Pea to continue.

"I know of your drive to do what is right. If Lighthive will bless this, come to our aid. In a week or so, we plan to fight against this deeply rooted evil. Hive Honey Quest, if cleansed, would be a powerful ally and friend to you in times of need." Pea took a breath. Love, Trust, Faith, and Peace were gawking at her, surprised. "I acknowledge that this is a great ask. I do not expect anything from you. But if you decide to help, it will not be forgotten. There could be a powerful alliance built between us."

The queen pondered Pea's presentation. "Ladies, you are granted our protection and lodging for the night. Rest your wings so that you may proceed on this mission tomorrow." She spoke slowly. "As for your boon, I will be considering this with my royal court. You will have an answer tomorrow before you depart. Return here at first light for our decision."

Sir Taves bowed, and he led the company out of the throne room. Wordlessly, they descended just below to an area that had many bee cells.

"What's a boon?" Peace whispered, having crept towards the front, next to Pea.

"A boon is a timely favor or request. Here, that is the word used when requesting something from the queen or her hive." Pea was looking forward. She had learned much in her adventures, and it was a good thing, too. This could be just the thing they needed to be victorious.

Peace was thoughtful. "Do you think they will heed our request?"

Pea turned to her comrade. "It could go either way. The hive has little to do with war, preferring peace. But yet, their drones are trained like warriors. If they believe in our cause, and see a benefit to themselves, they may decide to help. I am hopeful."

"It sure is good that you were the one to go with us on this search," Trust said quietly behind them, having listened in. "Without you, we never would have made this connection."

"If Hope weren't missing, I never would have thought of this, or ran into this opportunity." Pea muttered. "In a way, she is already leading us to... hope. It just looks a little different than you may expect." *Hope often looks different than expected.*

Their conversation halted when Sir Taves slowed. "Ladies, here are your cells. You will need to split into two groups. They aren't as spacious as you may be used to."

"Thank you, Sir Taves. Really." Love nodded toward the noble drone with gratitude.

"Kindness isn't considered a favor here, but a practice." Sir Taves smiled. "Be sure to convene just before sunrise. I'll meet you here, and escort you to the royal hall for your answer. You'll find sustenance prepared for you in your cells." With another bow, the noble drone turned and flew off.

Love looked at each of her friends. "I am usually the head of our group. But today, Pea, we would not be here if it weren't for you. Thank you. If it isn't obvious already, you are the one leading this mission. You may continue to act as such." She took a breath. "Tomorrow, when we depart, we will be heading straight toward the Mountain of the Sun, correct?"

Pea nodded, humbled. "Yes. I can lead you there. But know that your leadership still stands, Love. You lead well."

Love smiled. "So you have encountered this mountain before?"

"Yes, I have." Pea sighed. "I've been there once before. The problem is, I don't know how to find it again. I hope that the same inklings help me discover it once more. As I mentioned, the place seems to draw you in. That is why I think Hope may be there. Still, it's an uncertain journey."

The girls looked at each other. "Fair enough, I say. Are we ready to turn in? After such a long day, I am exhausted. I could sleep for a week." Trust spoke. The others agreed, suddenly reminded of their heavy fatigue. Before they trudged into their cells for the night, Trust added, "I don't know, Pea. Your brother Iris sounds like the kind of guy who would come around. If a war is to be had, I have a feeling you won't need to fight against your own blood."

HOPE HAD BEEN FLYING all day, and it was nearly dark. Her wings ached for rest. Scanning her surroundings, she spotted a hollow log on the ground that looked safe and suitable. She glided down toward the forest floor. After checking for predators, she settled into a patch of moss at the bottom of the log. It wasn't long before she settled into a deep sleep.

Hope's dreams were chaotic. *Where's Hope?* Her mother was panicking. *What about the prophecy?* Faith whispered. *We... we need her.* A voice echoed. After a brief and restless sleep, she awoke, tears in her eyes. Her mind was bogged with conflicting thoughts, and with a powerful homesickness. *Why would they depend on me?* Hope had buckled under the pressure. She had left the hive, flying in a straight line to the north, and she had gotten lost. She wasn't sure if she wanted to be found, or if she wanted to never be seen again. *How am I supposed to be what they want me to be? I can't! They have to be mistaken. I am no one special. I'm a young and inexperienced bee. I have nothing to offer. I'm scared. I don't want this!*

# Chapter 10: The Honeycrystal

Sweet Pea awoke with a start. Despite her anticipation of this morning's meeting, she had slept without disturbance. Besides, she had been much more exhausted than usual! Now, she felt refreshed. *It's early, but the sun will rise soon.* She woke the company, one at a time. After a quick breakfast, they assembled outside the cell doors as discussed. Within moments, a drone they hadn't met before arrived.

"Good morning. You have all been summoned to the royal court. I hope your night was restful." Wordlessly, the workers fell in line behind him as he took off upward. Their nerves were high. In a few moments, they found themselves standing again before the queen and her royal court. It turned out that Sir Taves was one of the court members as well.

"Sweet Pea, please step forward." The queen's smooth voice rang through the chamber. After a long moment, she continued. "My court and I have considered your boon."

Sir Taves stood. "Fellow friends, in the past, we have had many problems with the bees of Hive Honey Quest, particularly the drones. After failing at attempts to work with them, we retreated to our wood and receded our boundaries for pollination. We chose peace, and it has served us well. We grew strong like the oak we reside in." He took a breath. "Your boon has been considered and discussed, and we have made a decision."

Love and Pea exchanged a glance. It didn't sound good. *Here we go...*

"We have decided that we will help in any way we can."

The crew let out gasps in surprise.

"We have one concern. We have not communicated with your hive's queen, which is important. We must know that she is also of like mind. Right now, we only have your testimony."

Pea raised her hand to speak. "If I can respond? Due to the rushed nature of this rebellion, it may very well be impossible to have the validation you seek. If it means anything, you have my word. She fights for the cause. However, I know that you are taking a huge risk on our behalf." *Think Pea, think!* "We also don't know when the war will commence. May I present a plan, and see if it is of your liking?"

The queen nodded.

"When our battle begins, we will send a messenger bee to you immediately. As soon as you are notified, send a small party to the battle field, as well as your own messenger bee. Send your swiftest bees who can also be stealthy if necessary. We will send Queen Royal to an agreed upon meeting spot near the hive. When your party has confirmed the situation, one or all can return to you to relay their confirmation. If all goes well, then I pray, come as quickly as possible to our aid, and we will be forever indebted."

The council spoke quietly amongst themselves for a minute before Sir Taves spoke again. "We approve of the plan, and will help you fight against your oppressors. In return, we expect a peaceful and mutually beneficial alliance between both hives. We will help you win, so discussing failure is not necessary. Our party will meet Royal at the edge of Shadow Forest near the farm road." Sir Taves nodded at the workers and sat down.

Love could not contain her excitement. "Thank Lighthive, and thank you! We cannot adequately express how grateful we are!" A few tears escaped her eyes, as she landed on her knees. With that, the meeting commenced, and Sir Taves came to meet the group in the court.

"Congratulations. It will be an honor to fight for your freedom." He smiled. "Do tell, where are you off to next in search of your lost companion?"

"We believe it is possible our friend may be at the Mountain of the Sun. We'll be setting out that way immediately." Love answered.

Sir Taves looked surprised, and amused. "It just so happens that a few of us are headed that way today as well. We visit often, seeking guidance. We could accompany you on your journey, if you wish."

Pea nodded. "That would be most helpful, actually. I was led there once, but I'm not certain I could find my way there again. Your escort would quicken our step. Thank you." She paused. "How can we show our gratitude to Queen Shanelle, the court, and the hive?"

"As I said before, kindness is not a favor here, but a practice. Simply stand by our side as well, upholding your promise. That is enough." Sir Taves flew off, presumably to gather together those who would attend on their journey.

"Wow, talk about everything falling into place!" Faith was in awe.

"We have accomplished something great here today, but we must remember that our mission is to find Hope, and she is still missing. Today, we will need to cover a lot of ground. This battle should not begin without her!" Love reminded them. "Take these moments to rest, because rest will be scarce today."

The company rested and prepared for their departure, their faces lit with hope.

HOPE RUBBED HER EYES, disoriented. She had managed to get a few hours of sleep, and she was cooling off. Her longing for home intensified. She missed her friends, and her mother. *Why did I react so much? They must be worried sick!* She looked around, painfully aware that she was totally and completely lost. She had no idea which way to go to get home. *I am ready to face my fate. Whatever it may be that I must do, I will do it. Lighthive, I am a vessel. Send me as you please. Just help me find my way home.*

"Where will you go for answers, little one?"

Hope was startled to hear a bubbly voice above her head. Cautiously, she approached the sound, peeking her head out of the hollow log's ceiling. There, she saw a flashy butterfly standing with glorious golden wings that seemed to reflect every waking ray of sunlight. She rested delicately upon Hope's log, just a few inches away.

"I'm sorry, I don't... who are you?" Hope stammered, taking in the brilliant sight. She was completely awe-struck.

"I am Lightwing." The creature fluttered her wings, as if to display their intricate designs.

It was obvious this wasn't just any butterfly. Hope studied her for a moment. *This is... supernatural!* "Are you from..."

Lightwing nodded and smiled. "Hope, you need to follow the sun." With that, Lightwing took flight. Hope scrambled to follow her. Together they wove tirelessly between the trees for several minutes. Hope gasped for air, her lungs slightly restricted by her exhilaration. *This is probably the fastest butterfly that ever lived!* After sprinting about a beeline, they reached the edge of the cluster of trees. Hope gawked when she saw a huge, noble mountain come into view. It was too grand and tall to even fathom; it touched the sky. The sun was rising and had just emerged, illuminating its peak in a brilliant cascade of rays.

"Hurry, we must be on time!" Lightwing called. The mountain was bare of any trees because it was so steep. As they approached, Hope saw mist rising from a pool of water below. There was a beautiful waterfall spraying the gorge. Across the stream, a little meadow rested, vibrant and lush. The sun hit it at the perfect angle, and it looked to be out of the most pleasant of dreams. Hope was ripped out of her trance-like state as she was getting battered by intensifying winds, They grew more powerful as they began gaining altitude.

"I'm... struggling here!" Hope called ahead, as a wind current gripped her left wing mercilessly. She wasn't sure why the creature was leading her to heights that most insects would never want to experience.

"Almost there..." Lightwing showed no signs of stopping. They battled the winds and continued upward. "This way!" After what seemed like forever, they neared the steep peak. The air was thinner here and Hope struggled to catch her breath. Suddenly, there was a break in the cliff, and it leveled off. Lightwing landed expertly on the ledge, and Hope crashed next to her. Standing, she shook her wings that now ached with mild wind burn. Sighing, she peered across the flat toward an opening to what seemed like a network of peculiar tunnels. The cave entrance glowed with a faint, warm light. "Follow the sun." Lightwing gestured toward the cave, unmoving.

"Are you coming?" Hope asked.

"It seems I am needed elsewhere. Go on. When you find the crystal, you will be able to connect with Lighthive through dreams." And with that, she was gone.

Hope faced the cave skeptically. She entered the opening, only to find multiple tunnels. *Follow the sun...* Hope proceeded, choosing the tunnels that glowed the brightest. It was quite a tangle of paths. *It would be easy to get lost in here, especially at the wrong time of day.* Finally, she chose one more tunnel. This one was gleaming quite brilliantly. At the end, it opened into a larger room. The top of the cave was narrowly open to the sky, and in the center of the room lay a beautiful stone of rose quartz that was glowing ever so slightly. It was flat and smooth on its surface, and large enough to fit ten of her. Then, without warning, the room became very bright. *The sun is shining directly over the stone now.* It was so brilliant, she had to shield her eyes. *What should I do?* Without thinking, she approached the stone and touched it. It radiated with a pleasant warmth. She instinctually climbed onto the rock and laid upon its surface, and was gently drawn into a sleep-like trance.

# **Chapter 11: Hope is Found**

The company, Sir Taves, and a few others had set out together early in the morning on the grueling journey to the Mountain of the Sun. It was no small feat, that was for certain, but their escorts were clearly used to the journey. They had passed the forest's edge in no time and had approached a giant mountain and glorious valley. The girls had never seen adventure like this before.

As the group braved the battering winds upward, Love cried out. "This is impossible! No ordinary bee would be caught in these high winds." Still, they all pressed on silently, facing the impossible. Large gusts tore at their wings as they faltered and recovered. Just as it seemed like a hopeless battle, they toppled over as a current landed them on a flat outcropping. The air was silent and still here, without a hint of disruption, and a cave stood in front of them.

"We have missed the first light, but the stone will be lit for some time yet. We will still be able to connect with Lighthive." Sir Taves buzzed with urgency, taking the path without hesitation. He hastily led the group through many tunnels. The right one was so brilliantly lit now that it would be impossible to make a mistake. When they reached the crystal, the wild hive members climbed upon it quickly, paying no attention to the bee laying there already. Love noticed her though.

"Hope!" She rushed toward her, when Sir Taves grabbed her arm.

"Take caution! It is a shameful thing to disturb anyone when they are dreaming here. You would be best off joining us, if you find room. We will all awaken at the same time."

Hesitating, Love shook her head. "We will sit this one out. I think we'll return sometime. But now, I can only focus on our friend that we've finally found!" Her face glistened with joyful tears.

Faith stared at the stone longingly. "Yes, we will be back! We won't disturb Hope. Go ahead, Sir." The drone took the last large open place on the stone, and fell asleep like the others. Love, Trust, Peace, Faith, and Pea waited patiently for the bees to wake, not daring to make another sound. About ten minutes had passed when the dreamers began to stir and the stone's glow faded. The party waited anxiously for Hope to descend. The wild hive members filed off one by one and gathered in the room, quietly murmuring to each other. The last one to come down was Hope. She didn't seem the least bit phased to see her sisters, and was radiating brilliantly. It seemed that she was actually glowing.

Hope spoke. "*A powerful rising force shall be used to destroy the evil bees have fused, but there is hope that there will be peace for every kindred bee...* She recited, and continued. "*There will never be peace with evil in the hive. But when it's purged, love and peace will thrive. All will trust all, and faith will forever flow. This is the prophecy of Lighthive.*" The room was quiet as the company pondered these words. Sir Taves and his hivemates, while in their own sort of trance, looked on as well.

Sir Taves mumbled. "We call this *creetalle*, when we connect with Lighthive through the crystal and receive dreams and guidance. It is not guaranteed that you'll connect every time, but if connection is to be had, this is the place to make it quickly. The first time can be very disorienting."

Hope began rubbing her eyes as she became more present. "I have witnessed Lighthive like never before! I have been given wisdom for the war that is to come very soon." The light began to leave her face, and awareness replaced it. She paused, noticing the room full of bees. Finally she saw her friends, and a torrent of emotions exuded from her. "Love, and the whole lot of you!" Her eyes were grave. "You... are here. So far from home. I'm... sorry... mom must be so worried."

ROYAL WAS BROODING on her throne. Her thoughts were heavy as she thought of her many daughters on their dangerous journey. They had been gone for several days, and tensions were only rising in the hive as recruits were being collected. The hive's native bees had made much quicker progress due to their connections in the hive, and they had gathered many allies. *Will it be enough though?* Royal felt doubt creep in.

Other than these progressions, she had made her own strides. Since becoming queen and joining with a brand new king, her heart burned to win her mate to their cause. Ever since meeting him, she knew that something was different. He desired to please his father, and was still growing his own mind and convictions. But she could sense a goodness within him, and a desire for what is right. It was exciting to hope that he could be recruited. *It wouldn't be so scary to think of spending my life with him if we were of like mind. It may even be a blessing...* She had carefully tended a relationship with the drone, trying to build trust, and she knew she was so close to breaking through. Almost as if on cue, her king entered the throne room.

"Queen Royal. How are you?" He asked. While they were king and queen, things were still very new, and there was some awkwardness there. But, it was smoothing out, and even becoming endearing at times.

Royal attempted a smile. "Honestly, I feel the weight of the world on my shoulders right now."

Sting moved closer. "Is that something a Queen feels often, in a new hive, far from home?"

"Perhaps," Royal sighed. "Things are just more complicated right now. And with my daughters still missing, I am losing heart."

Sting was sympathetic. "Do you think they have found Hope? It puzzles me what may have happened to her. Bees are rarely lost here."

Royal had not yet revealed her doings to Sting, knowing she needed to be able to trust him first. And yet she was running out of time. Gazing at her mate with hesitant warmth, she suddenly sensed that the moment had come. Vibrations of urgency rippled through her abdomen, and she shifted uncomfortably as she tried to form the right words. "Sting... you are a good bee. You were not what I had expected."

Sting paused curiously. "What do you mean?"

"I was born here, Sting. And after I was shipped to a different hive, I fully realized how differently things are done here... how unnaturally. I never thought I would feel at peace about living beside a king for my lifetime. It's just not the way of bees. And yet, I am hopeful."

Sting hesitated, glancing into Royal's eyes. He waited for her to continue.

"At home, there is more freedom of thought. There is more respect to go around. Here, it pains me to see the mistreatment of many. Doesn't it pain you? Do you truly stand by these practices?"

Sting fumbled, not used to open discussion like this. "Our system makes us strong. Our honey production is very high, and our hive is well protected..." his voice trailed off.

"Sting." Royal insisted. "Are these flauntings worth the suffering at hand? Worth lives?" She stared at him, calmly. The same look Orchid bore that time in the throne room fell upon his face. Guarded terror. Royal knew that this was the moment, but she had to be delicate, or he may snap.

"For all of your life, you looked up to your father. He was strong and powerful, and he willed that you, too, would carry yourself with this strength. It was good, at first. You trained hard and became excellent. But then, things started to become more obvious. Your hivemates wore masks to conceal their trembling. They lived in fear. Even if you tried to address these things with Buzzz, you were punished for thinking this way. Am I correct?" Royal searched his eyes. "Sting, I don't claim to truly know your story. But I know that within you is a good soul, that would never justify Buzzz's actions or beliefs. You are better than this."

A peculiar look was on Sting's face as he contemplated Royal's bold words. After some time, he spoke quietly. "This is all I have ever known, Royal. This... is normal to me. It seems to work, you know?" He hesitated. Opening up wasn't something he'd done much before. "But to be truthful, there are small inklings within me that say otherwise. There are moments I... doubt our systems. I have even challenged them. You are right - I was punished. I was punished for even thinking there may be something wrong. So, I learned how to thrive here. I... have done horrible things, Royal." Sting's eyes misted. "I have given my life to this purpose. I fear it is too late, and too dangerous to consider anything else. I am tainted."

Royal's heart burned. "Sting." She looked at him with admiration. "You are very strong to speak on this." She paused. "And, you are the King. From here on out, your decisions must be yours. No one will carry the guilt of your decisions but you." She touched his hand. "It is *never* too late to do the right thing, Sting. You are never too broken or too spent to be changed."

His eyes were softening. Sting was unraveling. He no longer thought of being discovered.

Royal kept watch, but continued. "You need to be aware of what my friends and I have been planning. I don't expect you to join in the fight, but I beg of you to protect our secrecy. That is all I ask of you for now, if I am to make you aware of these things. Will you honor our secrecy?"

Sting nodded slowly.

Royal carefully explained everything that was unfolding. Sting was a bit guarded, but he soaked it all in without interruption. After explaining the plan, Royal paused. *He should know this.* "I also have reason to believe that your father... may have actually taken Lilac's life prematurely. This hasn't been confirmed, but there is evidence to suggest it. Perhaps he had some motivation, believing he could control you better than her... She still seemed strong enough, and Buzzz showed no sadness after her death... There is more, but no time to mention it."

Royal stopped when she saw Sting's face. Something had snapped in him, and his eyes were hard. "Unfortunately, that is believable." An angry tear escaped his eye. "Royal, I will maintain your secrecy. But I... need some time to process this conversation."

Royal nodded with understanding. *It's hard to know how he is feeling right now... It is as if his world is crashing down.* Wordlessly, Sting retired to his cell. He curled up into a ball and didn't move. The queen respected his peace, keeping quiet on her throne. Just mere moments after he became still, Buzzz walked in. Royal tried to hide her shock. "Buzzz." She nodded coldly.

"Royal." He dipped his head, almost mockingly. "Another day in the hive, another day as Queen. You ought to be honored." He puffed his chest with pride.

"Yes, it is not for the faint of heart." She looked at Buzzz blankly, like usual.

He shrugged before heading toward his cell next to Sting. Pausing, he turned back for a moment. "Royal, I think it is time we have a delegatory discussion. In the morning, we shall talk. The excitement of the hive's new king and queen is settling, and we must move forward in leadership as a united force." His voice was ambitious.

Something about his tone felt threatening, and Royal wondered what this would bring. *Do we need to act now? The time is nearing...*

# Chapter 12: Unfolding

Sting had contemplated more than he slept that night. His thoughts were dark and melancholy. *I would not be surprised if Buzzz did kill my mother. He wasn't too fond of her. This... is not okay. And yet, this is my life. Oh, how my world has been turned upside-down. Even just going along with things would be detrimental. I am forced to take a stand. A stand against all I have worked and trained hard for.* A tear escaped his eye. *I have to lay down my desire to please my father. I hate that he probably thinks he can use me. Through me, he thinks he will secure his superiority and power and enforce his new laws.* Sting would make sure that he didn't. Interrupting his thought process, his father appeared at the door of his cell.

"Sleeping in, now are we?" Buzzz hummed disapprovingly. "A king doesn't sleep in. Besides, we have much to discuss. Today, it begins." His lips parted into a twisted smile. "Royal's coming was timely, Sting. It was just the distraction we needed to shift into our final phase. Today, I will be enlightening the new queen. She will know her place in the new order of things. It is time."

Sting forced an expression of ambition and excitement. "When will this take place?"

"As soon as I find her," Buzzz scoffed. "It seems she is never in one place for long. That's one thing that will change."

Sting panicked inside. He recently was made aware of Buzzz's plan to implement an even stricter rule, and remove Royal from any position of authority. She was to lay eggs, and that was all. His father had been increasingly open about his plans since Sting had taken the crown. Buzzz had dropped the pleasantries more and more over the last few days as things started to come to a head. He knew that this was the moment. Things were about to break, one way or another. Would it be the reign of terror or the succeeding rebellion? Sting must have allowed his emotion to show on his face, and Buzzz looked at him oddly.

"Don't tell me you've begun to care for the girl. Remember, emotions are dangerous. They make you do things that don't make sense."

"Of course not. Have you seen her?" Sting joked coldly. "I can't believe that all you have trained me for is just moments away."

Buzzz nodded. "As you know, when new laws are implemented, there will immediately be a purge. Anybee who denies our leadership and resists our rule will be eliminated."

Sting concealed a shudder. "Do you think our numbers and training are sufficient? We must be sure that losing is impossible."

Buzzz's eyes lit with confidence and fire. "We will take care of anyone who dares to challenge us. No worries there. Our strength has grown to its maturity." He gleamed with evil pride. "Now, where is that girl?" Buzzz left in a huff, and Sting was left to his thoughts once again. *I don't choose this.* He gathered his wits. *In any way I can, I will help Royal... and the bees of this hive.*

NECTAR'S SPIRIT WAS full of anticipation. Today was special. She felt it in her wings. She was a very intuitive bee, as nurse bees often are. They bore a special link to Lighthive. *Today marks the beginning, or the end.* Nectar had stationed herself at the hive's entrance today in anticipation. Waiting patiently, she watched the sun as it peaked above the horizon. At that moment, Bebee, the hive's messenger bee, erupted into the grounds.

"Seven workers, a beeline off," she panted. "Approaching from the north." With that, Nectar took off to meet her sisters. She suspected that there would be drones waiting for them in the landing grounds beyond the hive's entrance when they returned.

It wasn't long before she intercepted them near the edge of Shadow forest. "Sisters!" The crew looked tattered and worn from their long journey. Nectar had suspected this, and she gestured for them to stop on a branch with her. "Rest, my friends. This may be your only moment of rest today." The company exchanged worried glances. Amidst them, Hope stood, self-assuredly. "Hope! You certainly have much to tell! And I am sure you all had quite the journey by the looks of you."

The girls huddled together, happy to be reunited for the first time in several days. After a moment, Love spoke. "Nectar, what is going on in the hive?" Her expression was somber.

"Girls, I believe that we have come to the breaking point. Your return couldn't have been more timely. You should prepare for war. If not today, I'm certain we will be required to take our stand by the end of the week. Buzzz has been laying low for a while, but tensions have been rising. I believe he intends to enforce whatever evil plans he may have very soon." She looked worried.

"Nectar," Love added, "you should know that on our journey, we were able to make an alliance. It will greatly add to our numbers. Perhaps it will be enough to win this fight."

Nectar's eyes flashed with hope. "Lighthive sure works in mysterious ways. I suppose we can thank Hope for her disappearance then." Hope was sheepish.

"There is much to tell." Love smiled. "However, our crew wouldn't have made this alliance without Sweet Pea. In fact, without her, I doubt we would have even found Hope. She was incredible." Pea lowered her eyes humbly.

Hope buzzed. "My friends... I am sorry for leaving without a word. I felt... overwhelmed. I am still young, and I felt the weight of the world on my shoulders. I felt I would almost explode. At that moment, fleeing seemed like my only choice. But in doing so, I put you all in danger. Forgive me. I am ready to do all I can to win our freedom."

Nectar touched her shoulder. "Hope, the good thing is, if we keep on correcting our path, Lighthive even uses our mistakes for good in the end. What matters is that you are here now. And with you, comes great news and great hope. We love you, and I understand how you may have felt. We are here to support you, and you are here to support us. Let us move forward with no qualms."

Hope's eyes were sparkling with grateful tears. "Thank you." After a pause, she added, "I miss mom. We need to get back!"

The company took a deep breath before taking to the sky. They didn't know what was lying ahead, but they knew that they were together. With them, was a deep love and joy that could not be tarnished. Something had shifted in them. They radiated with a new maturity and faith. As they wove through the trees, Hive Honey Quest was in sight. Nectar took a deep breath. *This is it.*

ROYAL PACED THE GROUNDS, uneasy. *Buzzz wants to talk to me, and I know it's not good. Come on, girls! I need you here!* She checked the hive's entrance again and again. As she continued to pace, a voice bellowed from the shadows.

"Royal! There you are! I have been searching for you all morning." Buzzz stepped into the light. "It's an hour past first light. You knew I was expecting you." He bristled. He wasn't as composed as she had been accustomed to. He began circling her.

"I apologize, Buzzz. Is a queen not free to wander and enjoy the morning?" Royal let her distaste show.

Buzzz sneered. "It's time to talk. I'm not sure what you are used to back home, but things are very different here, Queen. You are taking great liberty where there is none for you." He paused in front of her. "It's time you understand how things work here. Despite your title, you hold no power in this hive. You are subject to the power of the drones." A twisted smile broke upon his face as Royal shuddered.

*What is happening... Is it now? Are we ready?* "You are incorrect. A hive cannot survive without its queen. Its greatest task is to protect her, so it may continue to grow. A queen is respected and needed." Her voice wavered.

"Needed, yes." Buzzz said slyly. "Your job is to produce offspring, and that is all. I see no reason for you to ever leave the throne room." He paused. "Also, the well-being of your hive is your greatest concern. Therefore, anyone who doesn't serve the hive deserves no place here. Your daughters have little to offer. They are small and slow, like you." He added. "Yes, you are small. Definitely not ideal. As soon as we can, we will raise up new queens and select a successor-a daughter of Sting's that is strong. Then, you will be cast out. You will be nothing."

Just then, the company landed in the grounds beside Royal. Her heart fluttered to see her daughters. *How timely!* Gathering her wits and all of her height, Royal straightened. "I'm sorry Buzzz, but I will not step aside while you have your way with this hive."

He shook his head, unphased by Royal's retort. "Aha, just in time. All of you in one place," he hummed, satisfied. Then, several drones emerged from the shadows, trying to corner the girls.

"Retreat!" Royal took off explosively, her daughters following, toward the hive's entrance. They just barely made it past a large drone who tried to pummel them. They were disoriented and ruffled, not daring to look behind them. Royal knew that this was it. This was war. But she needed to get everyone on the same page first.

"I must go immediately to alert our allies that war is at hand," Pea blurted out, breathless. Without a word, she took off full speed toward the north.

Royal blinked, dazed. "Allies?"

"Yes! Good, right? They'll need to meet with you at the forests' edge to confirm you are leading this rebellion, and will honor an alliance after this aid!" Love exclaimed, out of breath. "Is this it? Is this... war? And are we ready?"

Royal panted, nodding slowly. "Yes. This is war." She paused for a breath. "My daughters, and Hope, I am so glad to see you all again. I just wish it were under better circumstances." She smiled weakly at her girls. "And we are as ready as we can be."

Hope spoke boldly. "Agreed. Now, it is time to destroy evil. And afterwards, we will have many stories to tell."

Slowly, bees began swarming out of the hive, drones and workers alike. Confusion gripped the hive, and no one knew what was going on. Disguised among the swarm were all of the recruits. There were many of them, but they were definitely still outnumbered. *We need to think smart.* Royal thought. *But with these supposed allies on the way to help, we might just make it.* Her eyes were filled with hope. *Lightive, be with us!*

# Chapter 13: Soldiers

Hope looked back at the swarm of bees, drones at the head. The enemy seemed to be taking formation and understood that a battle was at hand. *Fly like the wind, Pea!* Her head was spinning, and she was afraid. *Will this be my death? Our death?* She felt panicked as her thoughts ravaged.

"Hope!" Love blurted out. "Look out!"

Coming to her senses, Hope was almost slammed by a large drone. She darted out of his path. It seemed that the enemy was trying to strike, but with no apparent pattern or plan. It was chaos. Panting, she shielded her tool of death-her stinger. It was only to be used in the most dire of situations, as its use would kill her. Sending a quick prayer to Lighthive, Hope came to a sudden stop to confront the drones on her tail. Nearest to her was Clubb. Instead of approaching with confidence, he was faltering in flight. *These drones are caught off guard, unprepared. And they have no idea that in their midst, our recruits dwell. If we play our cards right, we will make it long enough for the allies to come to our aid. But, we need to sort out our recruits. It is dangerous for them to be mixed in with the enemies. They may not even know who is who.* Hope dodged a clumsy swing, snapping Clubb in the wing with her antenna. *Ouch!* Her whip-like blow caused Clubb to tilt in flight and drift downward, stunned.

Signaling to her sisters who battled nearby, the workers snuck toward a nearby branch in order to regroup. *We need to find our bearings. The recruits must gather.* She, her sisters, and various workers followed. They came one by one, trying to be inconspicuous. Some signaled discreetly to one another to spread the word. Before long, a large swarm of maybe a thousand bees rested on the hidden branch.

Love projected her voice. "Everyone, know your sisters! Know your cause! While there are some drones in our midst-take note of whom-almost every other drone is a target! We need to fight them before we fight any worker bees. We don't know everyone who's been recruited, and more still may serve our cause in the midst of battle. But we are currently outnumbered. Take care! We will ward them off, but it is also okay to lay low until help arrives!" Love shouted. The bees gathered there murmured. "You are all warriors, standing up to evil. You are all rebelling against tyrannical rule. If Lighthive wills it, we shall be free! We shall suffer no longer! Take heart, warriors. Be strong. Be smart. Let's do this!" The bees buzzed with determination. They began taking off in smaller groups, in every direction.

Nectar stood by Royal. "Your Majesty, while you may wish for it, you cannot partake in this battle. Losing you would be horrific. There are no eggs in the nursery cells right now. We wouldn't even be able to raise a new queen. After you touch base with the Hive of Soldiers, I urge you to come with me somewhere to lay low. Do you know where Sting is?"

Royal shook her head. "I don't. But he'll probably be expecting me to take shelter. We may be able to find him. I understand that I can't fight on the front lines. I know my duty. Stay with me, Nectar. Will you?"

"I will, my queen." After Royal and Nectar took off, the company exchanged glances. It was Hope, Love, Trust, Peace, and Faith.

"We need to stick together if we can," Love instructed. The sisters nodded gravely.

"May Lighthive be with us," Faith buzzed quietly.

And so it began. The war was starting, while informally. As the next several hours passed, various small groups moved about. They spent much of their time laying low, and otherwise attacked smaller groups or lone bees. The biggest goal was to stay alive until help arrived. Each small battle that broke out was very disjointed, with no rhyme or reason, making it mostly unproductive. But when the sun was high, Love stopped her friends.

"Look!" She pointed at a large, dark cloud in the sky. No, not a cloud. A swarm! "The wild hive has arrived!"

BUZZZ SCOWLED. HE HAD been observing carefully, and it was clear that Royal and her daughters were not the only bees turning against him. On top of that, his troops were clumsy. They had *planned* to have the upper hand. They had planned it all, but things were not going as expected. *All the same, I will meet my goals. They want war? Let them have it.* Buzzz had been training his drones in combat recently to equip them for such a time as this. He knew that as soon as they found their bearings, they would be hard to defeat. Buzzz knew they needed to regroup in order to create a new plan. He had been instructing drones here and there, but they failed to present as a unit. So he began signaling and gathering his army. The forest was sparse with bees, as many had taken to hiding, so he had no problem holding a meeting.

Clubb and Spade were among those gathered before Buzzz as he spoke. "Men. You are looking like fools on the field. Have you forgotten our months of training?" He scoffed. "Rise. Rise to the level you are. I know you can easily stamp out this little rebellion, and anyone else who gets in our way." He began pacing. "Listen. I have a plan. We will blind our enemies by terror." He raised a small pouch he'd retrieved from the stores about an hour ago. "We will make a ghost. The queen has a favorite daughter you see. If she is removed from the picture, we will take an easy win. She will be our spirit bee. On top of that, their little rebellion seems to take an interest in the spirit world. They should be easy to fool, and easy to take down when disoriented by their terror."

"What do you mean to do, Sir?" Spade was scratching his head dumbly while Clubb elbowed him in frustration.

Buzzz's face curled into that twisted smile. He opened the bag and dipped his hand inside. When he lifted it out, it was grayish-white, covered in chalk dust. "This will cling furiously to anything it touches. Who will make our ghost?"

HOPE WAS FLYING LOW, close to the forest floor. She had temporarily left her group to try and bring them something to eat. She also hoped to connect with the allies. She was pretty sure that the drones hadn't seen the swarm of Soldiers. *We have the element of surprise...* But suddenly, she was intercepted. An ornamented drone buzzed in front of her. "Ghost! I... see a ghost!" He made a face of sheer terror and sped off. Hope was startled and confused. *What the...*

"Flee for your lives!" A worker called.

A drone cried, "There, in the trees!"

In all of the confusion, Hope didn't detect the bee sneaking up behind her. She suddenly felt a dusting on her furry coat as a drone doused her with chalk powder. Unsure of what had happened, she turned quickly. She was not able to confront the drone or stop him, as he was already gone. Puzzled, she looked down at her hands. They were grayish-white and covered in powder. She tried to brush it off, but it wouldn't budge. She looked like a ghost - a real, scary story ghost. In every bush, voices called out "ghost" with alarm. *Ugh, this isn't fair!* Drones flashed past her with artificial terror on their faces. Hope called out. "It's me!" A few workers in the rebellion saw her, and screamed.

"It looks like Queen Violet!" One cried. They scattered, and there were lone bees flying blindly in any direction.

"It's me, Hope!" She called. She huffed angrily as she again attempted to brush off the chalk layer. Unfortunately, it had done its job and clung to her like a burr. On top of that, no one really knew her enough to recognize her differently. Few even knew her name.

CLUBB AND SPADE HAD joined a group in a thorn bush. Part 2 of the plan was ready to take place. Watching closely, they detected two lone worker bees close to the forest floor. Zeroing in on the she-bees, the group of drones descended quickly. *Easy pickings,* Clubb thought. They were almost on their targets before they could be noticed. One worker shrieked in surprise when she saw them.

"Be quiet you! It's too late now. Your carcasses will rot on the forest floor!" Clubb hissed. The loud worker didn't stop shrieking, as the other stood firm, ready for a fight. She tried to lash out but was unsuccessful. Before she knew it, they were surrounded. Just as Clubb was about to deal a final blow, a loud and angry buzzing pierced the air. They looked up to see a group of seven rugged bees, workers and drones. They advanced quickly toward the drones with righteous anger. Two of Clubb's group took off in fright, leaving only three. Clubb, Spade, and a drone named Arrow. Spade was trembling, as if in shock. "You'd better not leave me!" Clubb spat.

*You old savages, craving war,*
*We'll give you what you're asking for,*
*Death is what you dearly crave,*
*So let it be yours! None be saved!*
*Blood will stream, but not by you,*
*You can't touch our seasoned crew,*
*Try to hide and try to flee,*
*None can best a Soldier bee!*

Sir Taves chanted boldly as they closed in on the three drones. One of the workers they had rescued was none other than Pollen, Royal's dear friend. She joined the battle and fought boldly at the allies' side.

# Chapter 14: Warplan

One of Sir Taves' hivemates was an excellent craftsman. He was called Sir Bluffick. He crafted weapons like the spears they used, light armor, and the like. One thing he had crafted was a smooth stinger cover. It carefully fitted over a worker bee's stinger and came to a fine point at the end, allowing its wearer to use her stinger as a weapon without risking her life. Of course drones could not wield such a weapon, since they had no stingers. The wild hive had sparingly used such covers as an object of defense and attack. Soon, Sir Bluffick began to fashion them with a small opening at the tip, allowing for the wearer to sting their attacker without dying. A bee-on-bee sting will cause paralysis - sometimes temporary, and sometimes long-lasting, leading to death. So essentially, this cover made it possible for workers to fight like a queen honey bee, hornet, or wasp. These stinger covers were a dangerous tool in the wrong hands, but a powerful help for any who bore one. Sir Bluffick and some helpers had brought several of these covers to distribute among the workers of Hive Honey Quest's rebellion. Sir Taves gave one of the covers to Pollen after they won the first small battle.

"Thank you, this is quite a generous and helpful gift!" She dipped her head in respect. "You are all such a help. Without you, this war would be lost."

"We are pleased to help, and establish a strong alliance with the hive." Sir Taves smiled. "We don't have endless covers, but I wanted to make sure to equip Hope as well. Can you find her and deliver this?" He handed Pollen another meticulously crafted stinger cover.

"Absolutely." Pollen nodded.

"Great. Also, try not to use it unless you must. We'd be wise to lay low so they don't know what they are up against until it is too late." With that, Sir Taves and the group broke off to continue fighting.

Pollen carried Hope's cover as she began stealthily weaving through trees near the forest floor. *These may be our ticket to success and freedom.* She looked wherever she could without being spotted, with no luck. It wasn't until she neared the hive when she heard a scream.

"Ghost! Ghost in the field! Flee for your life!" Someone cried, shooting past Pollen's side. Looking around in confusion, she noticed that bees here and there were taking off in every direction instead of fighting. She glimpsed a lone worker getting snatched by drones from the bushes as she tried to escape what she had seen, but Pollen had to keep going.

*A ghost? What on earth is going on here?* With determination, she pressed on in the direction the bees were fleeing from. She squinted her eyes as she neared the treeline which opened into Alfalfa Hill. *Is that...* It did in fact look very much like a ghost. As she tried to make it out, she was nearly pummeled by Honey, Lilac's old nurse bee.

"Honey!" Pollen shouted. "What is going on here?"

"A ghost!" Honey looked terrified.

Pollen's expression was odd. "Honey, you are a nurse bee. We see the world differently, often seeing and hearing what others can't. Why are you so afraid?"

Honey took a moment to collect herself, as confusion fell upon her face. "You know Pollen, I'm not sure." She panted, peering past Pollen warily. "I... certainly should not be afraid. Right?" She shifted uneasily. "It has been so long since I have even been allowed to connect to the spirit world in any way. Perhaps I'm... rusty? But nonetheless, all the drones are terrified too! The fighting has pretty much stopped! I figure if the drones are afraid, I ought to be!" She shuddered.

Pollen tried to hide her amusement. It was all very clear to her. "Honey, have you ever seen a ghost? Much less, one who appears in broad daylight, unprovoked?"

Honey tipped her head. "Honestly, I've never seen one at all."

"For one, I doubt this "ghost" is truly what it seems. Secondly, this is all pretty odd. It seems clear to me that this was all spun up by the drones. I saw them bombard a worker not too far back. They didn't seem alarmed when they ambushed her from the brush!" Pollen flew forward just a bit, eyeing the "ghost". She approached until she could make out its face, and squinted. It quickly became clear that it was indeed no spirit. It was Hope, exactly who Pollen had been looking for.

Honey approached cautiously, letting out a sigh when she also recognized Hope. "Pollen, how do you have such a good mind for this? One would think you've seen battle before! In fact, very little seems to phase you!"

Pollen paused. "I'm... not sure. But, I think I may have an idea for how to regain the advantage in this battle. First, I need to talk to Hope. I have something of value for her."

SWEET PEA BATTED OFF her attacker. She shrieked as one snagged the edge of her wing, and she swiveled dangerously in flight. *I am so stupid! This was their plan all along! I should have never left my group!* Turning, she tried to catch a glimpse of her attackers, who had pulled her into a thorny bush. *Scar, Theo who is Thistle's brother, Scorch...* She parried another attack, almost unsuccessfully. *And who is that other one... Iris?!* She froze at the sight of the fourth drone. Iris was her own brother! He, of course, had always been more kind to her than any other drone was, due to their closer relation. She stared at him. Her body was in shock, refusing to do anything but hover helplessly. This very moment had been her greatest fear. She forced out the words with a squeak, "Iris! How can you do this?"

Iris gasped, having not recognized his sister at first. "Pea! I... I..." He ceased charging and slowed in flight. His comrades glared at him expectantly when he failed to deliver a final blow.

"Well? Where do your loyalties lie?" Scorch demanded, enraged.

"Come one, Iris! We work as a team... for Buzzz!" Theo called out.

Iris lowered to the branch and stood unmoving like a statue, temporarily unable to speak. He stared at his sister as tears filled his eyes. He slowly began shaking his head. "No. No, I can't do this. It's wrong. Pea, please forgive me..."

The other drones sneered angrily, charging toward Iris. Frantically, he projected, "Aaaarrraughhh!" Pea knew that cry. It was something Iris knew Thistle would recognize if he were nearby, since the two had been close friends before all of this. Iris's breath caught as he was pummeled by Scar, cutting off his cry. Pea watched, frantically flying here and there to look for an opening. The two were outnumbered. For a few moments they tried to hold their own, but they were losing, unable to keep up with their attackers. Pea didn't know if Thistle would respond to Iris's signal, even if he were in earshot. How could he be sure that Iris had good intentions? She dodged a drone, and prayed for help. Just before Scorch almost tore Iris's wing, Thistle broke into the bush without warning. He was holding a sharp twig in his arms, and without hesitation, attacked Scorch. He knocked the drone away from Thistle and turned back for more.

"You came!" Iris gasped, relieved.

"I believe in you, Iris." Thistle spoke quickly between blows. "I wasn't going to let you down, even if you were going to let me down." He flashed a smile at his friend.

Sweet Pea took this distraction as an opportunity to ram into Scar. "We are evenly matched now!" She announced confidently. *Thank Lighthive!*

During all of this, Theo had backed off discreetly so his brother wouldn't notice him. A minute passed, and Thistle, Iris, and Pea were gaining the upper hand. They had cornered Scar and Scorch between the crook of a large branch and the main stem of the bush. At that exact moment, Theo emerged from a shadow, and Thistle froze, stunned. "... Brother!"

"Brother! Don't do this..." Theo stood with a posture of defeat. When Thistle slowly approached him, Theo took his moment and pummeled into him, sending him spiraling downward. Theo flashed a proud smile, pleased by his performance. Sweet Pea cried out in distress, as the drones held her back from going to save him. Theo turned to her. "It seems that you are outnumbered, once again."

"You really care nothing about those who should be dearest to you..." Sweet Pea gasped, weak with hopelessness. But Thistle was not so easily diverted, and after a moment, he returned to continue the fight. Wordlessly, Pea, Thistle, and Iris resumed their efforts. The three worked together harmoniously, a deadly combination. They were determined to win this battle.

HOPE SIGHED IN RELIEF as she saw Pollen approach her. "Pollen!" *At last, someone here isn't completely bonkers!* Pollen rushed to her, giving her a quick hug.

"I am glad you are okay. You look crazy! What is this on you?" Pollen tried brushing the dust away, to no avail. "Anyway, take this. It's a gift from the wild hive to help us succeed." She handed the stinger cover to Hope, who stared at it curiously.

"How does this work?"

"I will explain shortly. First, we need to talk... about a warplan!" Pollen buzzed urgently.

"They covered me in chalk dust to make me look like this, and then pretended they were terrified of me! It was all just a diversion..." Hope was frazzled.

"Listen Hope," Pollen interjected. "Let's use their warplan against them with one of our own. I think I have an idea, but we need to communicate it to all of the rebels with speed and secrecy! We must work fast!"

"What is your plan?" Hope eyed Pollen expectantly. Honey was still collecting herself as the two conversed, eyeing Hope cautiously.

"The drones underestimate our wits. They want us to scatter, so that they can whittle us away one by one, right? Well, there's a way we can use this against them! Hear me out. Right now, groups of four or five drones are attacking lone stragglers. So, we need to form groups of at least six, each taking turns as the bait. A lone straggler, buzzing without direction. As soon as a group attacks the lone bee, the rest of our group races out of hiding to help. We will be able to overpower them, and they won't expect it." Pollen's expression was determined.

Hope nodded slowly in approval. "That makes sense. We need to spread this message promptly, or they might catch on too soon for it to be effective. We need many groups to do this at the same time." She looked down at her colorless appearance. "I'm going to need some help getting cleaned up. I'll be of no use while I look like this!"

# Chapter 15: Where is Royal?

After a long battle full of surprises, Pea, Thistle, and Iris were finally able to defeat Theo, Scar, and Scorch. They were a great team. While Thistle had refused to lay a hand on his brother, he proved very helpful against the others. Sweet Pea was talking seriously with Iris, but Thistle was not paying attention. He was too absorbed in his own troubled thoughts. *Pea is lucky to have a brother who loves her. During my days of apprenticeship, Theo was by my side the whole way. I suppose he may also feel betrayed by me...* A tear fell from his eye as he felt the sting of loss. *Things will never be the same. That's a good thing, but it won't be without difficulty to adjust. Sometimes I wish it were just me and my brother play-fighting on a sunny day. But now I have lost him forever.* He flew beside his friends blankly. Soon, they reached the edge of the forest overlooking Alfalfa Hill. A moment later, three workers raced toward them.

"Pea! Thistle! And... Iris!" It was Pollen speaking, Hope and Honey nor far behind her. She gave Pea a hug. She glanced at the convert. "I'm happy to see you on our side, Iris."

Iris dipped his head. "I'm ashamed it took me so long to find my sense."

Pollen's eyes were soft. "It isn't easy to let go of everything you've known. I am glad though." She paused. "Listen, we have a plan to regain the upper hand in this battle. We need to tell as many as possible, including the wild hive who came to help."

Before she continued, Hope suddenly piped up. "Hey, has anyone checked on Royal lately? We sent her to find safety, but it's almost dark again! Has anyone seen her?" The bees all nodded, concerned. "And my sisters?"

"We need to keep an eye out for them, but we also must focus on our priority, which is to win this fight! We need to..." Pollen was cut off as they all began hearing a loud buzzing sound. They heard a few horseflies whinny. Shocked, the group peered at the swarm not far off. It looked to be at least twelve bees, many riding captive horseflies. The herd approached quickly. Thistle had never seen anything like this before.

"It's the Hive of Soldiers!" Pea chimed. She rushed to greet them. "Horseflies, huh?" She glanced at the furious steeds who were clearly at their riders' mercy. She gulped, returning her gaze to the drones and workers. "Your timing could not have been more ideal! We have a plan to implement."

"That is good to hear." It was none other than Sir Taves.

"Sir Taves?" Pea searched their faces, seeing Sir Taves near the back. "It is so very good to see you. We can't thank you enough for coming to our aid."

"Have you ever seen a more noble cavalry?" He trotted his mount as he flashed a smile. He was evidently proud of this accomplishment. "We haven't had our chance to shine yet." He patted his horsefly's neck, and it snorted in disapproval. "We can ride like the wind on these, and they'll certainly be an unexpected surprise."

"Definitely!" Pea beamed.

Hope flew up to Sir Taves. "Have you seen a queen bee on your flight? We haven't been able to check on Queen Royal for many hours." Her eyes were filled with concern. At this point, the war had already been going on for two sunsets.

Sir Taves shook his head gravely. "I have not. I'm sorry." Behind Sir Taves, the craftsman called Sir Bluffick shouldered his way to the front.

"I have seen her!" He announced. The group gasped with relief. "While delivering weapons to anyone I could find, I spotted a queen bee. She appeared to be wounded, or distressed. She was very near to a large white box - your hive, I presume - resting on a wildflower.

With her was a worker, and a very large drone who crouched over her body, his head bowed." He sighed. "I did not have time to stop. They weren't painfully obvious, but they definitely weren't hidden either." Sir Bluffick dipped his head and steered his horsefly behind Sir Taves.

Pollen and Hope both had tears in their eyes. "What has gone wrong? She was supposed to find a place to remain hidden!" Pollen cried.

"She isn't dead, I know it." Hope forced herself to stand tall. "If she were gone, the war would have ended in our defeat." The others nodded.

"One way or another, Royal would want us to fight this battle and win." Pollen wiped her tears.

"We can't go to her now. That may even compromise her further. But we *can* enact our warplan."

Sir Taves smiled. "Fill us in. What is our course of action? I will communicate it to our other troops."

# Chapter 16: Devastated

Buzzz grabbed Theo's antenna and yanked him down. "Where is Iris?" He screamed.

"I told you sir! He's turned away!"

"Sure." Buzzz released Theo, causing him to stumble violently backwards.

Scar cautiously stepped forward. "He fought with us at first, but when he noticed we were fighting his sister..."

Scorch interrupted. "He said our way was "wrong", and betrayed us. He even helped to wound us." Scorch turned to display a fleshy tear in his abdomen. The gash was crusted and pretty deep. Buzzz turned toward Scorch and slapped his wound mercilessly. "Ouch! Hey! What's with you?" Scorch shot across the bush, fleeing Buzzz's angry hands.

"Be tough! Never complain... shut your mandibles!" He stated harshly, his rage spilling over. Gathering himself, he brooded. "Iris' departure is deeply troubling. It forces me to question the loyalty of each and every one of you. Who can I trust? How do I know that a simple stumbling block won't divert your path?" He stalked through the room, eyeing each drone he passed suspiciously. "Are *you* loyal?" He pointed at Scorch's face. "Will you be unwavering no matter how much it hurts?"

"Oh, sir, yes! Yes!" Scorch insisted, trembling.

Theo stood blankly with a hand on his head, his expression unreadable. Buzzz had ripped one of his antennae clean off. He had devoted his life to Buzzz and his plans, but he couldn't help but feel betrayed. He wasn't appreciated here. As each day passed, his leader's rage became more erratic. Buzzz was not afraid to murder in cold blood. He didn't have remorse, humility, or a care in the world toward those who defied him. But Theo had chosen where his loyalties lied, and was not the type to change course. Nothing could erase the hemolymph he'd already spilled in Buzzz's name.

Buzzz took off out of the bush in a huff. Clearly he'd had enough of them. "Buzzz is off his rocker..." a rough looking drone muttered under his breath.

Theo stayed quiet, looking down at the detached antenna in his hand. *He will kill who he doesn't like, and maim his friends.* Despite Theo's devotion thus far, Buzzz's recent intensity forced him reevaluate his loyalty. *I am too far gone for sure. Power doesn't appeal to me anymore, but peace will never find me. I am tainted. I am war-torn.*

# Chapter 17: Sideways

Sweet Pea, Pollen, Hope, Honey, Thistle, Iris, and a few Soldiers - Sirs Tamarack, Hauld, and Gareth set out on their quest. Hope was confident in this plan. Sir Taves led eight others as well, making two groups of nine ready to ambush. They had spread the word swiftly to all of the troops, so other groups were assembling as well. In the brief lull between events, Hope's thoughts drifted. *How can I bring hope to everyone? Will I have to die in this war?* She squeezed her eyes shut, grasping for the remnants of creetalle she'd experienced on the Honeycrystal. Almost like a far-off dream, she could only remember slivers of what once was. She saw Lightwing, the golden butterfly. Straining, she failed to make out the words the creature had relayed. *What is the point of the crystal if the encounter yields no wisdom?* Hope grunted with frustration. Still, a deep peace resided within her. It seemed to her that if the right moment came, she would have guidance to decide the next step. Somehow, Hope knew she was going to be a piece of their victory... that she would bring hope. *I don't know how, but I must be ready for that right moment.*

Pollen slowed behind Hope. "Okay everyone, Sweet Pea has volunteered to be our first straggler. She will signal us discreetly with her left antennae if she detects any enemies. However, we must NOT close in until they are in sight. She will fly in an open area where she and the enemies can be easily seen. Then, on cue, we will emerge from our hiding places and attack. After a few rounds, someone will switch out with her to be the new straggler." Pollen paused. "We need to conserve our energy if we wish to be largely successful. The quicker we can win these fights, the better. That is why we've selected groups of nine."

Love touched Pea's shoulder. "Be careful!"

Pea smiled. "I'll be fine; you have my back!" She was nervous, but ready to fight back and win this war.

"Right. Hope, Iris, Sir Tamarack, and I will take cover on the right. See those big leaves near the forest floor?" She gestured as the group nodded. "Honey, Thistle, Sir Hauld, and Sir Gareth should hide on the left in that hollowed tree. Both are close enough to respond in time, and both are far enough away to remain inconspicuous." Everyone took a breath and wore faces of determination. Pollen nodded to Pea. "Take your places!"

The group quieted as they discreetly hid themselves in the decided areas nearby. Pea watched carefully, and when they were all in place, she knew it was her turn. Taking a deep breath, she took off in the open. She purposely fumbled in flight while secretly eyeing every bush and tree. She flew in a jagged line with no obvious direction, acting lethargic. After a couple minutes, she spotted them - a group of five or six hefty drones erupting from a nearby rose bush. Pretending she didn't see them, she signaled the group with her antenna. Sudden fear gripped her chest as she realized these drones had no intention of leaving her alive. *Lightive help me!* She felt them approach speedily, closing in on her. Squeezing her eyes shut, she braced. *Our group is going to intercept them at the perfect moment. I'm going to be fine.*

Opening her eyes, she saw her comrades approaching rapidly. With renewed confidence, she raced toward the unassuming drones and pummeled one, who lost control and spiraled away. Just then, the rest of her group arrived to fight. The remaining drones froze in terror, looking as though they would try to turn tail and flee. But they were too slow, and bees collided with them before they could run. The Soldiers fought vigorously and were well trained. Pea stole glances with amazement between blows. Hope and Iris tag-teamed an enemy until he was badly injured and stumbling off. Pollen showed valor as well, fighting with bravery and confidence as the assumed leader of them all. She led well. Before long, the outnumbered drones were defeated.

Iris and Hope shared a high five. "We make a good team!" Iris buzzed.

Sir Gareth chased the last enemy into a thornbush before returning to the group.

"Good job, gang!" Thistle buzzed triumphantly.

"We fought smoothly! While one battle doesn't win a war, I think we can make a good dent at this rate." Pollen smiled.

"Have you battled before?" Sir Tamarack asked, his eyes showing admiration. "You have the presence and the wisdom of a general."

Pollen buzzed humbly. "I have not. Thank you Sir..."

Thistle piped up. "You should be our general. I can't think of anyone in the resistance who would challenge that idea."

"General Pollen, leading her troops with dignity, honor, and wisdom!"

Just then, Honey stepped forward to Pollen. "I, as a nurse bee, have had the privilege of assigning jobs and titles to many in the hive. So today, I honor you for your wisdom, humility, and bravery. You who are both a defender of good and a destroyer of evil, leading us with pride. Rise, General Pollen!"

Pollen's expression was awestruck. She dipped her head in respect and gratitude as the group began chanting. "General Pollen! General Pollen! General Pollen!"

"*Arrrghhh*!" A queen cried agony "Oh, I'm sorry. I don't usually feel such pangs."

"Keep on taking deep breaths," a small worker bee stated. "This delivery will be unusual. Something is... well, different."

A drone gasped. "What's the matter? Is something wrong?" Worry coated his gaze.

"Well, the egg has somehow gotten caught on something. It seems as though it is sideways. I have seen this before, but only once." she stammered, then murmured a silent prayer to Lighthive. *"We need your grace and wisdom right now."* Composing herself, she added, "I believe that everything will be fine."

"Are you sure?" The queen studied the worker's face with concern.

Closing her eyes, Nectar sighed. "I have peace. I believe Lighthive is with us to see this through." She gazed at Royal meaningfully. "Everything will be okay." Royal nodded, her fear melting away from her brow. Total determination and trust took its place.

Sting's wings twitched, doubt in his eyes. Lighthive was still a new concept to him, and he wasn't sure what he felt about it just yet. He shook his head and blinked warmly at Nectar, deciding to trust in her. "Thank you Nectar. You are a great nurse bee."

Royal bore down as another pang overcame her. She gritted her teeth. *"It is usually much... easier..."*

Nectar knelt beside her. "Let's try some new positions. Keep on breathing deeply." As Nectar continued working with Royal, Sting found himself slipping into a spontaneous daydream. He felt disoriented, as this had never happened to him before. First, he glimpsed a group of ten or so bees. They were all working together to attack a group of drones. Sting could recognize some of the bees in his vision. *Iris, Thistle, Sweet Pea, Pollen, Royal's daughter Hope, and others... fighting against Thorn, Seaquill, Tiger, Bone, Burr, Zeke, Peak, and Talon.* Before he could really make sense of the scene before him, it flashed to somewhere else. Four familiar bees huddled together, surrounded by four drones. *Scar, Scorch, Theo... Buzzz!* Sting had an overwhelming feeling that the workers were actually in trouble. This wasn't just an odd daydream. He blinked as his vision blurred and restored. He was back with Royal and Nectar. *What just happened?* Sting knew with certainty that he needed to tell someone about his vision. *Not Royal... She doesn't need to focus on anything this worrisome right now. But Nectar may know what to do... If I can pull her aside for a moment...*

# Chapter 18: Theo's Rebellion

"We are so glad you passed by our bush." Buzzz sneered at the small worker bees. "I know who you are. You are some of Royal's dearest friends," he paced in front of them threateningly, "which means only one thing. You must die!" The drones in the room erupted into shouts, snarls, and jeers. "You don't have any idea how long I've been patiently waiting to exterminate you from the hive. If it hadn't interfered with my plans, I would have done so immediately." Buzz took a long breath of anticipation. "But I'm not stupid enough to kill you while you're still so valuable. Oh the power we have now that you are within our clutches! No, for now, we will just make you as uncomfortable as possible. You will play an important role in this rebellion's ultimate surrender," he buzzed mockingly as his drones cheered again.

"You're a cold-blooded murderer!" Peace cried in disdain. Love, Trust, and Faith were huddled at her side.

"Correct." He turned to his nearest follower, Scorch. "While we wait, let us imagine how they will die. Won't that be fun? Now wait a moment, that reminds me of a scene that was woefully interrupted not too long ago. Perhaps you ladies remember." Buzzz smiled crookedly. "Men! Go gather enough birch bark to construct a small, *flammable* shelter. Soon, it will be time to finish what we began." His evil smile widened with glee, as though he couldn't wait to enact his devilish plan.

"And this time, there will be no mercy!" Scorch sneered, making a spark with a jagged stone. Then, he and Scar left the bush to begin scavenging.

"Theo, wait with the prisoners while I make their capture useful." Buzzz added, but Theo hesitated. His head ached where his antenna had been ruthlessly torn away. His anger was setting in, and he was about to crack. He tried to keep his composure, but Buzzz noticed his pause.

"Is something wrong Theo?" Buzzz stared at him furiously. He was not tolerant of hesitation. "You're no better than a deer fly caught in the headlights!" His expression changed to such scorn, it was impossible to ignore how deep it cut. Theo had been nothing but faithful for all this time, but it was clear that Buzzz didn't care for him in any way.

Something just snapped within Theo. "No, sir. I apologize." He effortlessly resumed an air of confidence, standing tall and bold.

Buzz circled him, suspicious. "Are you weary, drone? Are you weak? Can I trust your resolve, or will you falter, like a fool?"

"Sir, don't tell me you have begun to question my loyalty, or my strength! I'm not an idiot. I follow the strong side, and I persevere." Theo spoke defiantly with unwavering confidence.

Satisfied, Buzzz nodded. He strode past Theo, murmuring into his ear. "Make sure they aren't too comfortable, eh?" He glanced their way suggestively before taking off.

Theo turned to the four worker bees for a few moments. They were shivering with fear as he looked at them, his expression unreadable. He could have been pondering his secret thoughts of revolt, or plotting their intricate demise. Once they were certainly alone, he spoke. "Follow me, girls. We need to stay hidden." The workers stared at him with expressions of amazement, and suspicion. "Now don't just stand there and marvel! Come on!"

"Oh... uh, yeah!" Trust muttered.

"Who are you?" Faith asked warily.

"You don't know yet?" He buzzed gruffly. "I'm Theo, one of Buzzz's trusted right hand drones. Or... I *was*. We need to hurry if you want any chance of escaping." With haste, they followed him through a narrow, winding exit at the back of the bush. Thorns jutted out everywhere as the group wove through branches. It was clearly a way the drones didn't usually use. After a slow and careful exit, they discreetly flew along the forest floor to a large tree nearby and took shelter in its thick lower branches. They didn't dare to speak, nor to risk going further until they knew where their enemies were. After a few minutes, they could hear the drones dangerously close.

"I don't think I can carry any more bark," Scar buzzed, heaving under the weight of his armload. "We'll need to unload and make another trip."

"Yes. Where's Buzzz? Wasn't he nearby?"

Scar shrugged. "He seems to be on important business. Let's just head back to the bush now." The two drones huffed and puffed until they reached the bush with the materials. They landed with loud thumps on the thorny branch that Theo and his prisoners had just escaped. "Theo?"

"Get started on the birch shelter, okay Theo?" Scorch grunted. "Where is that dolt?" The two searched for a few moments before they were heard again. "You don't think... Scar?" His voice slowed warily.

"He wouldn't!"

"Scar. Theo and the prisoners are gone!"

"GREAT WORK, TEAM!" Pollen shouted triumphantly. Their group had just defeated another large group of Buzzz's followers, including some worker bees as well. They had garnered a few minor injuries along the way, but otherwise, were still battle ready. Hope had lost some fur, and one of her legs hung useless due to a pretty bad scrape. She pressed on though, with stubborn determination.

"Let's rest a little. Can we?" Honey pleaded, panting. The little nurse bee was not accustomed to roughhousing. Before she got an answer, Pea shouted.

"Hey, look!" she exclaimed, pointing at a small group of bees approaching. It was Theo and Royal's daughters, Love, Trust, Peace, and Faith. They looked ruffled and worn.

"Theo?" Thistle approached cautiously, his guarded eyes showing a glint of hope.

Theo approached the group, slightly sulking. His gruff appearance was amplified by his war torn coat. "Hey." The girls raced to Hope and Sweet Pea, their tears flowing as they embraced.

"What happened?" Hope cried. She held on to her dear sisters, fighting back her own tears.

"We were captured. Buzzz was going to use us as bargaining power." Faith's eyes were moist. "I think I've had more than enough life or death scares."

"It was Buzzz himself and some other drones, including... Theo. But he actually helped us get out of there!" Love added.

Hope eyed Theo suspiciously. Was this a trap of some sort, or had he really chosen to betray Buzzz directly? Something about Theo put her on edge, yet he seemed to be sincere. Shaking off her concern, she soaked in her sisters' hugs. She was filled with gratitude. "Then I guess we have Theo to thank."

Thistle approached Theo slowly. "Brother."

Theo was rigid. "I'm done with Buzzz. I hope that helping your friends can erase some of the woes of my past."

"Theo, we forgive you. It is never too late to choose a different path. Brother, I've missed you." Thistle gave his stiffened brother a quick hug. "We have a lot going on. We'd be glad if you could join our group for battle."

Iris had a reserved expression. He flew over to Hope, muttering. "Do you really think we can trust him? I've known Theo for a long time. He has been one of the most ruthless drones, even similar to Buzzz. That's why he was so trusted. He worked his way up to high command. I am telling you, I've seen some... horrible things." He wrung his hands nervously.

Hope shook her head. "We can't really trust him. But I suppose we need to give him a chance. He may surprise us all. But it wouldn't hurt to keep a watchful eye on him." Raising her voice, she queried. "Theo, do you know where Buzzz is hiding out? It is useful to keep tabs on him as much as possible for our own safety."

Theo dipped his head, hesitant. "...Yes. I do."

"Good."

Pollen straightened. "Well, everyone, we have conquered a large number of enemies thanks to the Soldiers' help and our warplan. I believe we have a real shot at winning this war." The group nodded in agreement.

Hope didn't hear Pollen though. She was in her thoughts when suddenly she felt a heavy pressure upon her. *I... I know what I must do. I can feel it! This battle cannot be won while Buzzz still stands. He must be exiled or destroyed. And I am the one who will do that. I see it now... this is how I'm the hope to fulfill the prophecy. It has to be me. I have to be willing to risk it all... and I am. I will risk everything if it means my friends can live in peace.* Her face hardened with resolve. *This is my role.*

# Chapter 19: Buzzz Must Leave

Hope sighed deeply. Her heart fluttered with anxiety, knowing the gravity of what she was going to attempt. *Buzzz must leave.* The thought tumbled in her brain repetitively. *Buzzz must leave. It's the only way.* It wasn't just instinct that told her this. It was her conscience, and it was guidance. *I can't do this alone. Lightive help me!* Hope moved with purpose. She had managed to speak with Theo to get Buzzz's approximate location. Then, she snuck off without anyone realizing. The commotion was distracting, but she knew they would notice her absence soon. She had to act now. *Buzzz must leave.*

The large, thorny rosebush came into sight. She landed on a nearby branch to watch, her heart racing. Breathing deeply, Hope waited as quietly as she could. She glimpsed two ragged drones erupting from the thornbush with intensity. After some confusion, they took off in opposite directions, probably to find Buzzz. Hope held her breath as she swooped down toward the entrance without the faintest sound. She was stealthy and quick, slipping into the door and concealing herself in the shadows and thorns. She waited. Moments passed like they were hours as she watched closely for her adversary to arrive.

"AND *push!*" Nectar used her hands to try to reposition the sideways egg. It was a painful thing to do, but it was all she could think to try at this point. Royal shrieked with pain as another cramp surged through her abdomen. The egg wouldn't budge. Nectar did her best to conceal her fear. Sting had made her aware of his vision, and it added to her worries. *When will this war end? Will I ever see my sisters again? Will this egg be Royal's end?* Her mind whirled. But she kept her demeanor calm, knowing that Royal could have no distractions. This was her duty now, and there was nothing else she could do. *Oh Lighthive! Please deliver! You gave me peace. I need you to act now!* Nectar kept trying to keep faith amidst these trials. She watched as another contraction subsided. "Royal, you are doing amazingly. Keep working. Lighthive will help you deliver this egg."

"I'm so... tired..." Royal sighed, depleted. "When will this stop? I am so... weak..."

Sting tried to soothe his queen. He looked as if he was sharing her agony. "Oh, Royal. This will all come to an end soon. This won't last forever." He stroked her head as she lay limp between the surges.

"Are you sure? I think I might just pass away." Royal forced a weak smile. "Or maybe I'm being punished for something."

"No, no. Not you. You have a heart of gold." A tear escaped Sting's eye as he gazed down with affection. "You are incredible." He hesitated. "Lighthive... Lighthive will be the strength you need to do this."

Royal looked at her king with warmth, soaking in his words. She glanced at the setting sun. "I've done all I can. Now you have to do the rest." She winced as another pang rushed over her.

"THEO? THEO!" BUZZZ roared. "Can I not even trust my adjutants? Fools!" He paced, chucking a shard of birch bark furiously. "What now..." He worked to calm himself so he could decide how to proceed.

After a few moments, Hope saw her chance. She emerged from the shadows to face the terrible drone. She stood tall and strong, not showing a trace of fear. "What's wrong, Buzzz?"

Buzzz turned as fast as a whip, his eyes flaming. "Ahhh, Hope." He stared at her, having taken no time at all to process this surprise. His lips curled into that wicked smile as he began circling her menacingly. "So, you decided to drop in. Do you expect me to die of fear?" He laughed mockingly, sizing her up. "What a match this will be. I can assure you, you will meet your end." He sneered. Not breaking eye contact, he snapped a narrow thorn from the bush for a weapon.

Hope concealed her stinger cover, returning his gaze unwaveringly. "Bring it on, drone. You won't scare me off." It took everything in her to hold her position, but she knew this was what she had to do. *Lightive help me!* She watched as Buzzz began pacing again. Suddenly, he shot forward to strike her with the thorn. She just barely dodged his attack. Recovering quickly, she turned to strike him on his back before spinning away. *I hope he didn't notice my weapon yet. I want to catch him off guard.*

Spitting, Buzzz turned to face her. He looked amused. "Well then, this will be fun!" The two circled each other, looking for the right moment to make contact. Hope worked to quiet her breathing and focus on the task at hand, until she was truly calm and centered. Just then, Buzzz launched himself at her without caution.

Hope saw this as her opportunity to deal a deadly blow. She ducked under the thorn he wielded and turned her back to him, with the intention of piercing him with venom. However, his response was so quick that he darted to the side. Hope had not been able to actually sting him, but she had managed to give him a nasty gash on his thorax. He fell to the floor, gasping for air. Pure hatred in his eyes, he stared at her stinger cover in frustration. He had clearly never seen one before, and didn't know how to defend against one.

Hope didn't hesitate. She took this moment of disorientation to attack. She flew toward him, stinger ready. He stood quickly and battered her to the side using the thorn. She gasped in pain where his thorn had sliced her abdomen. He then jumped on top of her, bringing the thorn to her throat. "And now Hope, you will die." He sneered down at her. "Any... last... words?" He struggled against her resistance.

Hope slowly stopped struggling, and became limp. She let out a breath, allowing fear and defeat to show on her face. "Tell... my mother..." Before she finished, she took advantage of Buzzz's lowered guard and quickly pierced Buzzz's abdomen with her stinger cover. He was completely shocked, as he slowly looked down at her stinger before he rolled off of her. Hope laid there, watching as Buzzz began to convulse. If she had gotten enough venom into his body, she knew this would be his end. "Tell my mother... that I did it."

Buzzz crawled desperately to the bush's entrance, and Hope was helpless to stop him. She lay there, the life draining from her body and her breath becoming shallow. Buzzz looked back at her smugly before rolling off out of the entrance. Below, she heard Scorch and Scar shriek. Other drone voices called out just moments later. Hope wondered if they would carry him away. She gripped her abdomen, wincing. *Is this how I die?* After a few moments, her vision began to blur. She saw glimpses of a drone's face before she lost consciousness.

DURING THIS BATTLE, in the very moment Buzzz was stung, Royal's egg moved. Why? It is a mystery. Perhaps it was justice that moved, or maybe, pure coincidence. Perhaps it was an unrelated phenomenon. But either way, it was something miraculous and unexplainable.

# Chapter 20: And There Was Peace

Sweet Pea followed Pollen gravely. After Buzzz's defeat and the warplan's success, the fighting dispersed. The resistance could claim victory. However, there was also great loss. The Soldiers were working together to carry Hope toward the hive on a soft leaf. Slowly, more and more members of the resistance came out of the trees to join them. Many carried their own wounded or dead. There was a chilling silence as they went forth in vigil. As Hive Honey Quest came into view, Sir Taves hesitated.

"General Pollen, this is where we must part." He bowed respectfully. "It has been an honor to fight at your side. We will uphold our alliance with pride."

Pollen dipped her head in gratitude. Pea flew up to them and spoke. "Sir Taves, this battle would not be won without your help." She paused tearfully. "Must you go this very moment? You will be dearly missed."

Sir Taves gave Pea a warm smile. "We must. Our troops also require rest and recovery. And Sweet Pea, if it weren't for you, we wouldn't have even had the opportunity to help. You are a huge part of this victory."

Pollen spoke solemnly. "Many moving parts have made this victory possible. Thank Lighthive, for they have orchestrated it all. Sir Taves, I extend our gratitude and friendship on behalf of Queen Royal and Hive Honey Quest." She paused. "We must all rest, and tend to our wounded. Go. And may you arrive home safely and swiftly."

Sir Taves smiled again, then gestured to his Soldiers. After transferring Hope - and with a few faint farewells - they departed. Sweet Pea looked on longingly. Her adventures had led her to many amazing friendships and experiences, but she had never thought those adventures would help save the hive. She glanced at Pollen with admiration. The General had led with wisdom and bravery. She had always liked Pollen, but she now saw her in a whole new light. Uncertainty gripped her mind. *I hope our queen is well.* Pea swallowed hard. If Queen Royal were hurt, or worse... the hive could be queenless and broken. Protecting the queen is every worker's greatest instinct, so it was very difficult to not know her whereabouts for so long.

As they approached the hive's entrance, the last ray of the sun's light dipped below the horizon, fading to darkness. They filed into their beloved home. As her eyes adjusted, Pea saw many familiar faces greeting her. She frantically searched for some faces that she could not find. *There are some friends I will never see again.* Such was the way of war. She waited in suspense as Pollen spoke up.

"Do we... have a queen?"

A worker named Petal answered her swiftly. "Yes. She is here, and she is well. Nectar and Sting have been with her."

"We must see her!" Love cried.

Petal nodded with understanding. "She rests in the throne room. She expects you."

Pollen, Pea, and all of Royal's daughters immediately made their way through the long hallways to Royal's throne room, carrying Hope. They drooped in exhaustion as they flew, but nothing would keep them from their queen. Before long, they were at her doorway, peering inside. There was Royal, cradling two small eggs in her arms. Sting and Nectar were at her side.

"Oh, Royal!" Love erupted into the room, tears flowing. "We have been so worried! You are okay!"

Royal looked up, her eyes alight. "My dearest friends! It is a relief and a joy to see you all!" Her eyes lowered to see Hope on the soft leaf. "Hope!" She cried.

Nectar rushed to Hope's side in response. She inspected Hope's wound carefully. "She is badly injured... but I think we can save her." She gestured for Royal's daughters to help bring their unconscious sister to a healing room. Sweet Pea and Pollen were left with Royal and Sting.

Royal looked solemn. "How is the hive?"

"It feels a little empty right now," Pollen responded sadly, "But the battle is won. Everyone fought bravely. The Hive of Soldiers came to our aid, thanks to Pea. Without them, defeat would have been imminent." She paused. "And Hope... she attacked and defeated Buzzz, which is the main reason we have the victory."

Sweet Pea spoke up. "Pollen was appointed General, and led us all with wisdom. Without her brilliance and organization, the win would not have been impossible."

Royal beamed at the two proudly. "Thank Lighthive! This hive is hurting... but we are free now. Free from the terror of Buzzz and his evil ways. Thank you for your service." She nodded at Pollen and Pea. "I welcomed two new hive members during the fight. It was a dangerous and painful endeavor... something was wrong. But suddenly, all was well and they were born. I thank Lighthive for that." She looked down at her precious eggs with affection.

Sting spoke. "We have welcomed a new drone and worker today. Our first children. Royal and I have chosen to name them Courage and Joy, to represent the battle for freedom and victory!"

"It's perfect." Pollen stated warmly.

*A powerful rising force was used,*
*To destroy the evil bees had fused,*
*Hope fulfilled the prophecy,*
*Of peace for every kindred bee.*
Or - at least - they were well on their way.

*THE END*

# Don't miss out!

Visit the website below and you can sign up to receive emails whenever Amarah Parks publishes a new book. There's no charge and no obligation.

https://books2read.com/r/B-A-YPKX-NRVMC

**BOOKS 2 READ**

Connecting independent readers to independent writers.

# About the Author

Amarah enjoys a quiet life in Minnesota with her amazing husband and adorable one year old son. In addition to writing, she enjoys creating and releasing music as well as raising competetive show rabbits.

Read more at https://www.instagram.com/amarahparks/.